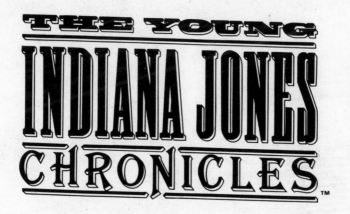

THE YOUNG INDIANA JONES CHRONICLES™

Revolution!

D1367957

Adapted by Gavin Scott

from his teleplay "Petrograd, July 1917"
Story by George Lucas

Directed by Simon Wincer

With photographs from the television show

RANDOM HOUSE 🏠 NEW YORK

This is a work of fiction. While Young Indiana Jones is portrayed as taking part in historical events and meeting real figures from history, many of the characters in the story as well as the situations and scenes have been invented. In addition, where real historical figures and events are described, in some cases the chronology and historical facts have been altered for dramatic effect.

Copyright © 1992 by Lucasfilm Ltd. (LFL)
All rights reserved under International and Pan-American Copyright Conventions. Published in the United States by Random House, Inc., New York, and simultaneously in Canada by Random House of Canada Limited, Toronto.

PHOTO CREDITS: Cover and interior photographs by Jaromir Komarek, © 1992 by Lucasfilm Ltd. Map by Alfred Giuliani.

Library of Congress Cataloging-in-Publication Data
Scott, Gavin.
Revolution! / adapted by Gavin Scott ; story by George Lucas ; directed by Simon Wincer with photographs from the television show.
p.   cm. — (Young Indiana Jones chronicles ; TV-6)
"Adapted by Gavin Scott from his teleplay 'Petrograd, July 1917.' "
Summary: Caught in the middle of the Russian Revolution in Petrograd in July 1917, Indiana Jones tries to keep his student friends out of trouble without betraying his involvement with French military intelligence.
ISBN 0-679-83238-6 (pbk.)
1. Soviet Union—History—Revolution, 1917–1921—Juvenile fiction.
[1. Soviet Union—History—Revolution, 1917–1921—Fiction.
2. Adventure and adventurers—Fiction.]   I. Lucas, George.
II. Title. III. Series. PZ7.S4245Re 1992
[Fic]—dc20   91-51201

Manufactured in the United States of America   10 9 8 7 6 5 4 3 2 1

Revolution!

INDY'S TERRITORY IN "PETROGRAD, 1917"

0   100   200 Miles

NORWAY

SWEDEN

FINLAND

★ Petrograd
(St. Petersburg)

North Sea

Moscow

GREAT
BRITAIN

Baltic Sea

RUSSIA

GERMANY

FRANCE   SWITZERLAND

AUSTRIA-HUNGARY

Black
Sea

Chapter 1

"Whose side are you on, comrade?" demanded the soldier, pushing the young foreigner against the wall of the Pushkin Theater. Half a dozen other soldiers closed in around him, cutting off all hope of escape.

Indiana Jones saw that the men were from the Machine Gun Regiment. Many of its members were misfits who had been kicked out of other units. It was one of the most extreme and violent groups in St. Petersburg. And there were more groups in the city than Indy could count!

Indy chose his words carefully. "I've only been in Russia a few weeks," he said. "Who am I to tell you what sort of government you should have?"

"You're right, comrade," said the first soldier, clearly pleased with Indy's answer. "But *I* can tell you. We've gotten rid of the Czar. Now the land must go to the peasants. The factories must go to the workers. And power must go to the people!

"Take a leaflet," he added, thrusting one into Indy's hands. "It explains everything. Comrade Lenin himself will speak at a meeting tomorrow. If there's anything you don't follow, Lenin will make it crystal clear!"

"Don't forget! We'll be looking for you," said another soldier who was about seven feet tall.

"Great," said Indy, trying his best to smile. "Thanks."

The first soldier slapped Indy's back cheerfully. Then the soldiers set off down the street, handing out leaflets right and left.

Indy sighed with relief. The fact was, if those soldiers had known what Indy was *really* doing in St. Petersburg in the middle of the Russian Revolution, they'd have shot him.

It was July 1917, only a few months after the

Russian people had chased Czar Nicholas II off the throne. Nicholas had led Russia into the Great War with Germany and made a complete mess of things. Casualties were horrifying. And at home, the people starved.

After the Czar was kicked out, a Provisional Government was set up to run things. The country remained at war. The new Minister of War, Alexander Kerensky, did not want Russia's allies to abandon her just because a revolution had started. But many people wanted the troops to come home *now*. And soldiers were deserting in large numbers.

Russia's allies, France and Britain, needed to know what the Russian people were going to do next. Indy was one of the spies who'd been sent to find out. For cover he was a cultural attaché to the French Embassy. His knowledge of languages had gotten him the job.

It sounded glamorous, but most of the time Indy was stuck in the embassy basement decoding messages from the agents who were out where the real action was. He compiled their information into reports for his boss, Monsieur Laurentine. Of course, Indy wanted to be out in the field himself. He spent every spare moment wandering through the streets of the city, trying to find something important enough to free him from that boring basement.

St. Petersburg had been renamed Petrograd at the start of the war, but everyone still called it by the old name. By any name, it was a magnificent city. The river mirrored lovely parks and fine buildings. Wide, handsome streets were lined with palaces, theaters, churches, department stores, and cafés. Colorful trams rattled noisily along the boulevards. Horse-drawn cabs clattered across the bridges that joined the city's hundred and one islands. And with a deep breath you could smell the sea air from the Gulf of Finland.

All of St. Petersburg seemed to be out in the streets these long summer days. Everyone had an opinion about what should happen next in Russia. Everyone had a poster to put up, a leaflet to hand out, or a speech to make. The cafés were always full of people shouting, laughing, and calling for more tea to wash down their heated discussions.

As Indy watched the soldiers disappear, he caught sight of the big clock on the City Hall tower. Ten minutes to ten o'clock. Oh no! He was going to be late for work again! Reluctantly, he hopped aboard a tram.

An armored car with a red flag waving from its round metal turret zoomed out of a side street. Indy watched it overtake the lurching tram. The car was full of Machine Gunners, off to spread their message: The land must go to the peasants, the factories to the workers, and the power to the people.

They're up to something, thought Indy. But so was *everybody* in St. Petersburg. They had a world to remake!

The French Embassy was a large, elegant building not far from the center of the city. It had once been the palace of some member of the Russian nobility. The peaceful, tree-lined square in front of it seemed a million miles from the excited turmoil of the rest of St. Petersburg. Indy hurried through the great iron gateway, showed his pass to the guard, and dashed up the handsome steps of the old building and through the massive gold-and-cream-painted front door.

His footsteps echoed as he ran along marble halls, then leaped down stairs two at a time. The nearer Indy got to his office, the narrower the stairs became—and the less marble there was. By the time he reached the basement, grandeur had been replaced by the bare essentials.

As the office door closed behind him, Indy felt trapped. This was partly because the small room was packed with files, books, maps, posters, and papers from floor to ceiling. But the main reason was that Pierre Brossard was sitting across the table from him.

Pierre Brossard, the other member of Monsieur Laurentine's intelligence team, was a sleek young man with small, round, wire-rimmed spectacles. Pierre Brossard was always tidy, efficient, and punctual. He made Indy grind his teeth.

"Ah, Captain Défense, so glad you were able to join us," said a voice from the shadows behind Brossard. It was Monsieur Laurentine himself.

"Henri Défense" was the name Indy had adopted when he first joined the army. It happened to be the Belgian army. The United States was still staying out of the Great War, but Indy wanted to be where the action was. Actually, Indy was too young to join any army then, so he invented a new identity. When he saw a French "No Smoking" sign—*"Défense de fumer"*—it seemed like a good joke to use Défense for his name. But since enlisting he had served on the battlefields of Flanders and Verdun and in the deadly jungles of the Congo, and the joke had begun to wear a little thin.

"Sorry I'm late, Monsieur Laurentine," Indy said, combing his brown hair with his fingers. "I was keeping an eye on the demonstrators in the streets."

"Especially the pretty ones," said Brossard, not quite under his breath.

The look Indy gave Brossard would have burned him to a crisp, if Brossard had been at all sensitive to murderous looks.

"We have field agents to keep an eye on the demonstrators, Captain Défense," said Monsieur Laurentine. With his spectacles and neatly trimmed beard and well-tailored suit, he was a preview of Brossard in fifteen years. "Your job," he continued, "is to study the reports those agents send us and come up with conclusions.

"Remember, we have to find out if the Communists—or Bolsheviks or whatever they call themselves—are going to try to take over the country anytime soon. Just imagine what it would be like if there were no private property!

If everything from factories to farmland belonged to 'the people'! Communists! The very word makes me shudder!"

"I think the Communists are on the move, sir," said Brossard confidently. "I've had a dozen reports of arms being ferried into the city."

Indy jumped in at once. "Brossard, you were telling us the Communists were going to try to take over the government weeks ago! The Communists talk big, Monsieur Laurentine, but they're in no shape to take over Russia. I wouldn't worry about them. They just don't have enough support."

"But we can't afford *not* to worry about them, Captain," said Monsieur Laurentine. "France and Britain want the Russians to go on fighting against Germany. If the Bolsheviks take over, they'll pull the Russian troops out of the war."

"That's one of their strongest selling points, Défense," said Brossard. "Lenin is promising to bring the soldiers home! Have you any idea how that sounds to somebody who's been stuck in a trench at the front?"

"Don't tell me about the front, Brossard," snapped Indy. "I've been there. But that doesn't mean the Bolsheviks are going to win."

"My analysis suggests—" began Brossard, and got no further before Indy interrupted him.

"Sir, can Brossard get on with his analysis on his own? I'd rather be out in the field collecting the facts instead of arguing with him about what they mean."

"The facts are no use without analysis, Captain," replied Laurentine sternly. "Your Russian is excellent. You decode well. I need you here."

"But, sir," said Indy.

"And I'd appreciate it if you could get to work on time for once. Captain Brossard never seems to have your trouble with being punctual." And with those words Monsieur Laurentine left for his comfortable, airy office upstairs.

"You've got some nerve, Défense," said Brossard. "Why should Laurentine let you out in the field instead of me?"

"Because I am a natural field agent, Brossard, and you are a natural . . . desk clerk!" said Indy. He sat down and looked gloomily at the pile of paperwork before him.

"Huh!" replied Brossard. "There's only one way you'd be of use in the field—as a scarecrow on a farm!"

To emphasize his point he crumpled up a piece of paper and threw it at Indy's head. But Indy caught it neatly, then flipped it open. When his eye caught the message on the paper, his mood changed abruptly.

"Hey, when did this come in?" Indy asked.

"Our man in the Preobrazensky Regiment passed it in early this morning," said Brossard, puzzled.

"Look, hold the fort for me, would you? I've got to go out for a half hour," said Indy, jumping to his feet.

"Go out?" yelled Brossard. "You just got here!"

"This is an emergency," said Indy.

"I don't have time to do your work, Défense," whined Brossard. "There's a whole load of . . ."

But Indy was already through the door.

"Thanks, Captain," Indy called. "I knew I could rely on you."

And he was gone.

Chapter 2

Indy looked like an Olympic athlete as he sprinted out of the embassy. He took the basement stairs three at a time and skidded along the marble hallways toward the main door like an ice skater. The grave, dignified embassy servants looked on in shocked disapproval.

Then disaster loomed. Just as Indy reached the door, it opened to admit the Ambassador himself and his entourage of secretaries and under secretaries. The First Secretary closed his eyes to avoid seeing the awful collision. But at the last minute the Ambassador stepped aside. Indy, hardly noticing him, dashed right through the door and leaped down the front steps in a single bound.

Slightly shaken, the Ambassador raised an eyebrow.

"It's good to see not all our young men believe diplomacy means a life of ease and leisure," he said to the First Secretary.

But Indy was too far away to hear him. He was racing across the crowded square. He pushed past soldiers and wove through groups listening to speakers. Then he turned into the narrow streets that led back home, his heart thudding in his chest.

For a poorly paid young spy, Indy lived in a rather grand building. Until recently it had been the town house of an aristocratic Russian family with great estates in the country. But the family had fled when the Czar was overthrown. Young students whom Indy had met in his expeditions around the city had taken over the building. They'd divided up the huge rooms into little alcoves for themselves. When they'd invited Indy to join them, he'd accepted gratefully. It wasn't easy to rent an apartment in St. Petersburg.

The building wasn't in quite the shape it had been in when one family owned it. The big staircase leading to the upper floor where Indy and his friends lived was usually dark. Indy stumbled several times as he raced upward. He ran along the dimly lit hall at the head of the stairs, pulling open doors.

"Sergei! Irina! Where are you?" he yelled.

But there was no reply. All the rooms were empty. Indy heaved up a window and leaned out. Looking down into the next street, he saw his friends. They were carrying a large red banner.

"Sergei! Irina! Stop!" called Indy at the top of his voice. "I said—STOP!"

But they were too far away to hear him. Indy slammed the window down again and ran back the way he had come. Seconds later he was dashing out of the building and taking a short-cut through an alley to a broad avenue. Indy could see Irina and Sergei's banner bobbing above the masses of people. He barged through the crowds until he ran right into the broad back of a young man wearing a tattered soldier's uniform. All the insignia were torn off, but a red arm band had been added.

"Hey, watch where you're going!" said the

man. But his anger changed to delight when he saw it was Indy. "Irina," Sergei shouted to a young woman with long, light brown braids wound about her head. "Look who's come to join us!"

When she turned, her pretty face lit up with pleasure. "Indy! I knew you wouldn't be able to bear missing Sergei's speech. But what is it? You look like you've seen a ghost!"

Irina was a literature student at the university. She came from a well-to-do, middle-class home. She'd only been caught up in the excitement of the revolution when she'd met Sergei three months before.

Sergei knew what the revolution was all about. His family were factory workers. They'd slept on the damp floor of the hemp factory where they worked because they didn't earn enough to rent their own place. Two of Sergei's little brothers and sisters had died when they were young. Sergei had watched his parents turn into old people before his eyes.

When Sergei was sent to the front to fight the Germans, he found the war was run as badly as the peace had been. There was no more concern for the soldiers than there had been for the workers.

One day a Bolshevik asked the men in his unit why they didn't simply throw down their rifles and go home. Sergei found no reason not to.

Now Sergei was back in St. Petersburg. He was working to bring the Bolsheviks to power and stop the war for all the soldiers. And Irina, because she loved him, was helping. She wrote essays for her literature professor by day and pamphlets for the Bolsheviks by night.

"You're going to the Tauride Palace, aren't you?" panted Indy. The Palace was the seat of the government.

"Of course we are," said Sergei. "I want those fools in the government to understand how the ordinary soldier feels about this stupid war. Didn't you hear me rehearsing my speech all last night?"

"Somebody's got to tell them," said Irina. "We've got to stop this war!"

"Listen to me," said Indy, still breathless. "Don't go near the Tauride Palace this afternoon."

"Why not?" demanded Irina, astonished.

"I have to go, Indy," said Sergei. "You know that."

"Not today," said Indy. "Believe me."

Sergei and Irina looked at him, completely puzzled.

"But *why?*" repeated Irina.

"Because you're a deserter!" hissed an exasperated Indy.

Sergei stared at him. "So?"

Indy's brown eyes slid sideways. How much could he tell Sergei without betraying the informer who'd passed on the message Brossard had thrown at him?

"The Tauride Palace is going to be a dangerous place for deserters today," he said.

"How do *you* know?" demanded Irina.

Indy bit his lip. "You know I can't tell you that," he said. "Just—trust me."

Irina and Sergei looked at him doubtfully. Sergei had been working on his speech for days.

"Hey," asked Indy. "Are we friends?"

Sergei grinned. Warmhearted and impulsive, he'd liked Indy ever since they'd first met in a shop doorway during a drenching rainstorm. Indy had whiled away the time telling him stories of his days with Pancho Villa and the Mexican Revolution.

"Of course we're friends," he said.

"Then you promise you won't go?" insisted Indy.

"All right. I promise," Sergei said at last.

"Good," said Indy, smiling with relief. "I've got to get back to work now. See you tonight at the Bearpit."

And he disappeared into the crowd.

Chapter 3

That night an exhausted Indy pushed open the door of the Bearpit café and surveyed the scene before him. Every time he came here it amazed him. It was as though all Russia had been squeezed into one huge, smoky room. The Bearpit sold tea, vodka, and ale. The tea was brewed in samovars, huge gleaming copper urns covered with fancy decorations.

Waiters wearing white Russian blouses, buttoned up one side to the neck, ran back and forth. Dodging elbows and toes, they carried bottles, glasses, and plates of sausages to the hungry, thirsty, shouting customers. A huge lantern with "The Bearpit" written on it hung in the center of the room. Every inch of wall space was covered with posters urging people to support this or that party or fight this or that enemy. A blind musician was playing an old Russian folk tune on a concertina. A grubby peddler went from table to table with a tray of old clothes. A crippled beggar wheeled himself about the floor asking for alms.

There was so much noise and chatter, you could hardly think, let alone see your friends. But as Indy peered into the murk a friendly voice sang out.

"Hey! Indy! Come and have some tea! They just filled the samovar!" called a young woman named Rosa.

Indy smiled and pushed his way through the tightly packed tables. Rosa was a medical student with a pleasing, open face. Dmitri, the thin, undernourished young man seated next to her, had been studying to be a priest when the revolution broke out. When the Czar was in power, priests were important. Russia was a very religious country. Now Dmitri's future didn't look so bright. But he kept on attending classes at the seminary, hoping the revolution was just a temporary upset.

Rosa had seen too much suffering at the hospital where she did her training. She didn't think much of the war or the Czar who started it. But unlike Sergei and Irina, she didn't think Russia should turn to the Bolsheviks to replace him.

Now, however, all Rosa was thinking about was Indy. Her face lit up as he sat down between her and Dmitri. She loved the way Indy knew so much about the world—and history and literature. When she borrowed one of his books, she devoured it as if it were a meal she'd been wanting for months.

Rosa handed Indy a book he'd lent her just three days ago. It was by H. G. Wells, the great science fiction author who wrote *The Time Machine* and *The War of the Worlds*. But like so many authors these days, Mr. Wells was now writing about what sort of world there should be after the war.

"Thank you so much for lending me *War and the Future*, Indy," said Rosa. "It was full of terrific ideas."

"So you think Mr. Wells is right? Should there be just one government for the whole world?" asked Indy, grinning. "I'm not sure I agree."

"Well, I do," said Rosa. "If there were just one government, countries wouldn't be fighting each other all the time. What's the sense in that?"

Dmitri joined the argument. All he wanted was to go back to the time—just a few months ago—when the Czar was on the throne, the priests were in their churches, and everybody did as they were told.

"Look, Rosa," Dmitri said. "These writers— H. G. Wells, George Bernard Shaw, even our own Maxim Gorky—think they know how to build paradise on earth. But it's not possible, because people aren't perfect."

"Why isn't it possible?" demanded Rosa. "*Anything* is possible now! The Czar is gone, Russia is free. *We* decide what happens next!"

"No, we don't!" protested Dmitri. "God decides. And if you try to force people to create paradise on earth, all you'll end up with is a huge amount of suffering."

"Nobody's going to *force* anybody to do anything," said Rosa. "The Provisional Government will hold elections within a month or two. Then people can make a free choice about what sort of government they want."

"If the Provisional Government gets a chance to hold elections," countered Dmitri.

"Of course they will," said Rosa. "Who's going to stop them?"

Indy, like Dmitri, wasn't as sure as Rosa that those elections would ever be held. But before he could respond, Sergei and Irina had pushed their way through the Bearpit crowd to join them. Sergei walloped Indy forcefully on the shoulder.

"Well, Comrade Spy," he said jovially, "I took your advice. The crowd at the Palace didn't get to hear my brilliant speech. Instead Irina and I spent a very boring afternoon folding leaflets. I hope you're satisfied."

"You made the right choice, Sergei," said Indy.

Indy didn't like Sergei calling him a spy in front of all these people, but all he could do was treat it as a joke. He'd never told Sergei he was a spy, but Sergei had guessed.

"Maybe this'll make up for your disappointment," Indy said.

He reached into his pockets and began bringing out some slightly squashed food that he'd "borrowed" from the embassy. Food was short in St. Petersburg these days.

"Butter!" said Irina, grabbing it. "We haven't seen butter for weeks!"

"And rolls!" yelled Sergei, hugging Indy. "Hey, Spy, I love you!"

Sergei shoved a roll into his mouth and began to chew furiously. The others followed suit. Indy laughed.

"If the French Ambassador knew he was supporting a gang of revolutionaries, he'd have a heart attack!" Indy said.

But in fact only Sergei and Irina were really revolutionaries. They were convinced that Bolshevism was the only path Russia should take. Like them, Rosa was glad the Czar had been overthrown. But she wanted people to be able to choose for themselves, through elections, what the new Russia would be like. And Dmitri—well, Dmitri dreamed every night that the Czar was back in his palace and Russia had returned to the way it had been for the past thousand years.

The sort of revolutionary who would really have given the French Ambassador a heart attack was coming into the Bearpit at that very minute. Boris was an anarchist. He didn't believe in *any* kind of government. He thought people could get along perfectly well without officials telling them what to do. He was supposed to be studying agricultural engineering.

But ever since the Czar was overthrown, he'd been running around the city all day and all night—organizing demonstrations, preaching about anarchism, and generally getting himself into trouble.

Big and stocky, Boris had messy hair and the beginnings of a beard. He was very funny and very exciting to be around—and a bit danger-ous. Tonight, for example, he was covered in blood and clutching a large bottle of vodka. His friends stood up in alarm as Boris lurched toward them.

"What's happened, Boris?" cried Rosa.

She reached into her bag for something to wipe away the blood.

But Boris shrugged her away. "It's all right, it's all right! There's nothing wrong with me! Look, vodka! How long is it since we saw vodka?"

"Last night," muttered Dmitri.

Rosa doggedly began cleaning the gash on Boris's arm, using the vodka as an antiseptic.

"Where were you, Boris?" asked Sergei.

"Where do you think?" demanded the anar-chist. "Waiting for you to make your speech outside the Tauride Palace! You Bolsheviks are all alike—completely unreliable. One thing you can say for anarchists—we're punctual!"

Boris grabbed some of the food Indy had brought and started wolfing it down.

"So what happened?" asked Irina.

"A gang of soldiers turned up," said Boris. "They started picking deserters out of the crowd and arresting them! They said the deserters could either go back to the front and fight the Germans—or get shot. I'm telling you, there was blood everywhere."

Irina and Sergei knew now why Indy had been so determined Sergei should not make his speech at the Tauride Palace.

Irina put her hand over Indy's.

"How do you spies find out all this stuff?" she asked.

"Come on, Irina," said Indy. "We have an agreement, don't we? You don't ask me what exactly goes on at the French Embassy. I don't ask you exactly what goes on at Bolshevik Headquarters. We may be in opposite camps but we're friends, right?"

Rosa looked up from dressing Boris's wound. She was puzzled.

"But why did *you* get into a fight with the

soldiers, Boris?" she asked. "You're not a deserter."

Boris let out a huge, booming roar. "Oh, I didn't hurt myself fighting the soldiers! That rotten shop window did this a few minutes ago, when I was getting the vodka!"

Everyone burst out laughing. Boris grabbed the bottle back from Rosa.

"Stop wasting it!" he yelled cheerfully. "This is for our party!"

And as everybody applauded, he took a great swig and slapped his belly. Tonight was a night for fun!

Several hours later, Indy and his companions swiftly left the café, stumbling onto the pavement. The door was slammed shut behind them.

"That's the fourth time Boris has gotten us thrown out of a café in ten days!" said Rosa.

"You'd think people would enjoy a good discussion, wouldn't you?" said Boris.

As usual, Indy's friends had started arguing furiously—and happily—with everyone around them. Was it right that some people should be rich and some poor? Did a country need capitalism to be prosperous? Should people be made to share wealth if they wouldn't do it willingly?

Would democracy work when millions of voters couldn't even read? In fact, the friends were discussing the same things people all over the city were discussing.

"People like a rational discussion, yes," said Dmitri, looking embarrassed. "But Boris—why did you have to throw the samovar at the proprietor?"

Boris didn't hear him. He'd opened the door of the Bearpit again and was shouting a few last words to the assembled customers. *"Don't write us anarchists off too soon, you cretins! This is a revolution we're having—not a tea party!"*

"It *was* a tea party when Boris threw the samovar!" shouted Rosa, running across the road.

The others followed her through an alley and ran right into a short, round, middle-aged man in a bowler hat. He was striding along the pavement, waving his arms furiously.

"Police! Where are the police?" he yelled. "I am Nicolai Bogucharsky, a respectable citizen. And I want the police now!"

"There *are* no police now, Mr. Bogucharsky," said Rosa. "We got rid of them when we got rid of the Czar. Don't you remember?"

"What kind of a country is this without a

police force?" demanded Nicolai Bogucharsky. "Who's going to uphold the law and order?"

"Would you rather have the Czar back?" asked Irina, just as fiercely. "And nobody free to do anything?"

"Never mind the Czar," said Bogucharsky. "Who's going to get those women out of there?"

'What women?" asked Irina.

"Us!" shouted a voice above them.

Indy and his friends gazed upward at a three-story building. "Bogucharsky Shirt and Blouse Factory" was painted in large letters across the brickwork. The front door had been barricaded shut. But women were leaning out of all the windows. They were excited and triumphant. Many were waving shirts, blouses, and rolls of cloth.

"We've taken over the factory, Nicolai Bogucharsky," called out one woman. "It's ours now!"

"*Yours*, Ekaterina Suvarov?" Bogucharsky shouted. "Who worked for years to find the cloth and buy the machines and sell the shirts? That factory is mine! I never treated you badly. What right have you to take it away from me?"

"Because we're the people who make the

shirts! And now that the Czar's gone, who's going to stop us?" asked Ekaterina.

Irina saw her chance.

"Hey! Let me in!" she shouted. "I've got some leaflets from Lenin I want to give you!"

"What's Lenin going to do for us?" Ekaterina was suspicious.

"Let me in and you'll find out!" Irina answered.

"You need to be organized if you're going to survive!" said Sergei. "Irina will help you."

"No, no, no!" yelled Boris. "That's the last thing you want! You have to make your own decisions. Don't let some Bolshevik tell you what to do!"

"I want my factory back! NOW!" yelled Mr. Bogucharsky, beside himself with rage.

Rosa and Indy exchanged smiles. They both knew the argument would go on for the rest of the night.

"This is really interesting," Rosa said. "But I'm on duty at the hospital in fifteen minutes. I've got to go."

"Me too," said Indy, determined not to be late for work next morning. "I'll walk with you. It's on my way."

"Great," said Rosa as a pile of newly made nightshirts sailed out of one of the factory windows and landed on Nicolai Bogucharsky. The last thing Indy and Rosa heard as they rounded a corner was the muffled voice of the industrialist crying, *"This is an outrage! I will not stand for it!"*

Chapter 4

The next morning Indy felt slightly the worse for wear after the previous night's partying. He sat bleary-eyed at a huge polished table in the Ambassador's conference room. It was in a part of the embassy he rarely got to visit—the upper rooms. There were huge oil paintings on the wood-paneled walls and rich carpets on the floor. Everything was elegant and orderly.

Indy ran his fingers through his hair in an effort to make himself as tidy as the surroundings demanded. Or at least as tidy as Pierre

Brossard. Brossard always looked as if he had just come to work via a clothing store and barbershop. Indy sometimes wished he could dump a few pounds of sugar on Brossard's well-oiled hair.

Half a dozen diplomats sat around the table. They all stood up when the Ambassador entered. He was in full ceremonial uniform, complete with sash and medals. Nodding briefly, he gestured to them to sit down, and came immediately to the point.

"Gentlemen, as you know, ever since the Czar fell Russia has been ruled by a temporary government of honest men. This Provisional Government is determined to hold free elections so that the Russian people can decide on their future for themselves." The Ambassador paused. "I've just come from a meeting with the Provisional Government. I have to tell you—in the strictest confidence—that I seriously doubt whether it can hold on to power until the elections."

A current of surprise electrified the listeners, with the exception of Monsieur Laurentine and his two young spies. They'd suspected it for some time.

"The problem is Lenin," said the First Secretary. "Ever since he came back from exile, he's been telling the people the Provisional Government is little better than the Czar. It simply isn't true. The fear is he'll get people so agitated they'll overthrow the government before there's time to hold elections. Lenin and the Bolsheviks could just take over! The next three months are crucial."

"Alexander Kerensky, the Minister of War, thinks the Bolsheviks will attempt a coup within the next two weeks," said the Ambassador. "If he can find out exactly when they plan to make their move, he'll be able to do something to prevent it. The Provisional Government is desperate for information."

Giving each man a piercing glance, the Ambassador continued. "I promised that the French Embassy will do everything it can to help. I expect you all to work with the utmost diligence. I don't have to tell you how important it is to France that the Provisional Government *not* be overthrown."

"Remember," said the First Secretary, "the Bolsheviks have promised to pull Russia out of the war. Then millions of German troops will be free to attack the Allied forces on the battle-fields of France, where they may well overrun us. That's how much is at stake in this matter."

"I might add that there will probably be a promotion for whoever provides the information we need," said the Ambassador. "Or at least a more attractive assignment."

Indy could hardly contain his excitement. If he could find out the date of the Communist uprising he could get out of that basement and prove himself the field agent he knew he could be. His eyes met Brossard's. They both realized they were thinking exactly the same thing.

It was early evening in the house Indy shared with his young revolutionary friends. Their huge room upstairs looked like the camp of an eccentric group of desert nomads. Great em-broidered quilts were strung from the ceiling to divide the room. Indy had made himself a sort of tent in one corner with a large Turkish carpet. A chandelier still hung from the center of the ceiling, but it no longer held candles, only dust. A giant four-poster bed with elaborate carvings and decorations dominated one side of the room. This was the base for Sergei.

At this moment Irina was slicing cabbage beside an old stove. Sergei was at the table painting a new slogan on their old banner. Yesterday's slogan was out-of-date now. On the floor was a poster Boris had been drawing. It showed a landlord trampling on a peasant.

Boris was particularly good at drawing bloodthirsty posters. Whether he drew a cruel landlord, a greedy capitalist factory owner, or a heartless general ordering his men into battle, the villain always looked like Boris's Uncle Pavel. He had once beaten Boris with a stick for stealing apples. Fortunately for him, Uncle Pavel lived hundreds of miles away in the country. If he were ever unwise enough to visit St. Petersburg, he'd probably be lynched on sight. Boris's posters had already convinced everyone that Pavel was the worst man in Russia.

Sergei was just finishing his banner when Rosa arrived.

"Hi!" she said, a little self-consciously. "Is Indy about?"

"Should be," said Irina, throwing some cabbage in a pot. "It's his cabbage."

"Can I help?" asked Rosa.

"You can peel the potato," said Irina, grinning. There was just one potato for them all.

"On second thought, just wash it. We don't want to waste the peel. We'll bake it in the oven instead."

As Rosa busied herself with the potato, Irina spoke to her softly.

"You should speak to him, you know. It's no good just staring at him like a sheep."

"Who?" said Rosa, closing the oven door.

Irina looked at Rosa and raised an eyebrow. Rosa blushed and giggled. It was no good trying to hide anything from her friends.

"But surely he realizes," Rosa said. "He must!"

"Rosa," said Irina. "One thing you've got to understand is that men are really stupid."

"Unless they're wise, liberated young revolutionaries like me," said Sergei from the table.

"*Especially* if they're wise, liberated young revolutionaries!" said Irina, throwing a dish towel at him. "They're the dumbest of all!"

The door opened again and Indy and Dmitri came in.

"Hey! That smells good!" said Indy, looking in the pot. "Here's something else the Ambassador won't see on his table tonight."

He pulled a large, round loaf out of his knapsack. Irina was absolutely delighted.

"That's perfect!" she cried, grabbing it from Indy and putting it aside. "*Just* what we need!"

"Great!" said Sergei as he removed his banner from the table. "Hey, let me have a chunk!"

"No!" said Irina vigorously. "It's not for now. We have to save it."

"Save it?" said Sergei, puzzled. "But I'm hungry *now!*"

"Sergei! Come *on!*" said Irina, looking at him meaningfully.

"Oh yes. That's right," he said, not sounding at all convincing. "I *don't* want to eat it now. I'm not *at all* hungry."

The conversation made little sense to Indy. But he was too busy reading Sergei's banner to care.

Irina quickly brought out a plate of pickled herring. "Come, everybody, eat some herring until the stew's done," she said. "This should keep you quiet, Sergei."

Sergei grabbed the chair Rosa had been going to take beside Indy. When Irina kicked him hard on the ankle, he finally got the idea and went to the other side. At which point Boris burst in, shoved *his* chair between Rosa and Indy, and started wolfing down the pickled herring. As usual, having a full mouth didn't stop Boris from talking.

"Hey, things are really buzzing out there, you know? I haven't seen people so worked up since we threw out the Czar."

The bag Boris had been carrying slid down beside his chair and spilled some leaflets onto the floor. Indy picked one up and glanced at it casually.

"One of the priests at the seminary said he's heard the Bolsheviks are going to stage a coup within the next ten days," said Dmitri.

"Really?" said Indy without thinking. "Know anything about that, Sergei?"

"Hey, Comrade Spy! Remember our deal?" said Sergei, taking a playful swipe at Indy.

Their eyes met. Indy hadn't forgotten their deal at all. But he was desperate to get out of that basement.

Suddenly a loud explosion made everyone jump.

"What was that? A bomb?" asked Dmitri.

"No," said Rosa, pointing to the oven. "I forgot to prick the potato before I put it in to bake!"

Everyone burst into relieved laughter.

After supper Indy and Sergei played chess.

Boris and Dmitri sat beside them and gave them what they were convinced was useful advice.

"Oh no, you shouldn't have done that, Indy!" shouted Boris. "Total disaster! You're finished now."

"Check," said Indy to Sergei, moving his bishop.

On the other side of the room, Rosa and Irina were putting dishes away.

"I don't know if I can go through with this," whispered Rosa.

"You can do it, I know," said Irina. "You know how to hold his attention."

"I don't think I do," said Rosa unhappily.

"Listen, Rosa, the key is confidence. All you have to do is keep him away from the apartment until nine o'clock."

"I'll try," Rosa said with a sigh.

There was a whoop from the chess table.

"Checkmate!" shouted Indy.

"Capitalist swine!" yelled Sergei. "How did you do that?"

Indy just smiled. Then he got up from the chess table and strolled over to Rosa and Irina.

"Hi, ladies!" he said cheerfully. "Conspiring?"

"You men are always so suspicious!" Irina

said. "I have no time to conspire. I have to write an essay on Charles Dickens tonight for my professor and a leaflet about giving land to the peasants for my boss in the Bolshevik propaganda department."

And she picked up her books and went out, giving Rosa a meaningful look. Rosa drew a deep breath and gathered together all her courage.

"Indy, there's a Mozart recital at the Conservatory tonight," Rosa managed to say, although her mouth was dry with nervousness. "They're playing the Concerto for Clarinet and I was wondering . . ."

"The Clarinet Concerto?" exclaimed Indy, delighted. "Rosa, you know the way to my heart! Shall we both go?"

"Yes!" she said, beaming. "Yes—I'd really like that."

Rosa sighed with relief. She'd brought it off. Not only had she plucked up the courage to ask Indy out for a date, but she'd also made sure Irina's secret plan would work.

Indy didn't notice Rosa's smile. He was busy studying the leaflet that had fallen out of Boris's bag. It had given him an idea.

"Look, Rosa," he said. "I have some things

42

to do first. I'll meet you at the Conservatory in an hour."

"Wonderful," said Rosa, looking at him with shining eyes.

But Indy was already halfway out the door and down the stairs. He'd had a brilliant idea.

Chapter 5

For the next half hour Indy hurried around the streets of St. Petersburg, peering at poster-covered walls and slipping into cafés to check out the noticeboards. He tore off loose posters where he could and copied down the details where he couldn't. Normally he tried to avoid people who wanted to give him badly printed leaflets about upcoming marches. Now he gratefully accepted everything he was offered and stuffed it into his pockets. Laden with this strange loot, he checked in with the guard at the gate of the French Embassy.

Minutes later he was at the table in the basement, arranging his collection into piles according to the date and place of the event being promoted. Suddenly he became aware of a dark figure by the shelves at the far side of the room. He leaped up, then sat down again, feeling a little foolish. It was just Brossard.

"Putting in a little extra time, Captain?" said Brossard, amused that he'd given Indy a scare.

"I suppose you haven't even gone home yet," said Indy grimly.

"Of course not," answered Brossard. "I'm going to find out when the Bolsheviks plan to start their uprising and get that promotion. Going home early is out for some time."

Indy gritted his teeth and got back to work. He pulled a calendar toward him and started circling dates on it, checking them against the piles of leaflets. Brossard watched him for a moment and then turned back to the shelves.

Thirty minutes later, at half-past eight, Indy was waiting outside the Music Conservatory.

"I'm sorry I'm late, Indy," panted Rosa as she hurried across the square. "I—"

She stopped as she realized something was wrong. The building was closed and dark.

"The concert's been canceled," Indy said sadly. "The orchestra was sent to the front to entertain the troops."

"Oh! That's awful!" gasped Rosa. "I'm really sorry, Indy."

And she was. Not only was she not going to hear Mozart, but now the conspiracy was in serious danger. She had to keep Indy away from the apartment until nine. Otherwise—disaster!

"That's okay," Indy replied. "In fact, I'm really tired. I've been running all over the city collecting stuff and I'd like an early night."

Rosa's jaw tightened. This was terrible. She thought quickly.

"All right!" she said. "But first, there's something just near here that I really want to show you!"

"Another night, Rosa," said Indy firmly. "I want to get home."

"No, I insist," said Rosa, steeled by desperation. "You'll love it. It's just around the corner."

She took Indy by the arm and almost dragged him. A few minutes later they were standing in front of a small humpbacked bridge.

"There!" said Rosa. "Isn't it beautiful?"

Indy looked at the bridge. It was quite a nice little bridge, but it was just—a bridge.

"Yes! It's fine!" he said politely. "It's really pretty. Thanks for showing it to me. Well, I've got to get going now."

"There are hundreds of bridges in St. Petersburg, Indy," Rosa said enthusiastically. "All different and yet all somehow—the same!"

"I guess so," said Indy, thinking how nice it would be to take his boots off and go to sleep.

"There are short ones," said Rosa keenly, "long ones, wide ones, narrow ones, stone ones, wooden ones, straight ones, humpbacked ones. Every kind of bridge you can imagine!"

"That's wonderful," said Indy. But when he started to move away in the direction of home, Rosa took his arm.

"You see, when Peter the Great decided to build this city, back in 1703, there was nothing here but a bunch of islands in the River Neva," she said. "A hundred and five, to be precise. He brought the best architects from all over Europe to create the most splendid buildings in Russia. And he joined the islands with over seven hundred bridges!"

"I'll always remember that, Rosa," Indy said, starting to leave again.

"You're going the wrong way," said Rosa. "There's a shortcut through this alley."

"You sure?" said Indy doubtfully. It didn't seem the right way at all.

"Of course I'm sure," said Rosa. "I was born in St. Petersburg. And if we go back this way, we can pass a bridge with four gilded griffins on it! They're really something."

At eight-fifty they were standing beside yet another bridge. Rosa was even more enthusiastic about this one.

"See the turrets?" she said. "Very few bridges have turrets like that. They're so picturesque. Peter the Great slept in a log hut while they were building the city. He wanted to supervise every detail. It was still a great wild swamp then. Two of the guards outside his palace were eaten by wolves as late as 1725!"

"Rosa, are you *sure* this is the way back to the apartment?" asked Indy.

"No, I made a mistake," said Rosa cheerfully. "It's this way. But the good thing is we'll get to cross a bridge with the most amazing cast-iron railings!"

Indy had been brought up to be a gentleman,

especially where ladies were concerned. But he was seriously considering picking Rosa up and dropping her right off one of her beloved bridges.

At nine-fifteen Indy and Rosa were crossing their sixth bridge.

"You know, you could write a book about the bridges of St. Petersburg," said Rosa brightly.

"I don't *want* to write a book about the bridges of St. Petersburg, Rosa," said Indy. "I want to go home! I'm sure that if we take that street over there, we'll be back in five minutes. Let's follow *my* directions for a change, huh?"

Rosa looked at her watch, then fumbled in her pocket.

"Oh no!" she cried. "My purse!"

"What?" said Indy, stopping in his tracks. "You've lost your purse?"

"It was so silly of me," said Rosa. "I think I know just where I dropped it, too."

"And where was that, Rosa?" Indy asked, doing his best to control his temper.

Even Rosa was embarrassed by what she had to say.

"By the . . . Conservatory," she admitted at last.

"Where we started?" said Indy tightly.

"Where we started," repeated Rosa.

Indy drew a deep breath, said nothing, and started walking.

At nine-thirty they finally arrived back at the Conservatory. It was still broad daylight. St. Petersburg was so far north that the sun hardly seemed to set in summer.

Rosa bent down and appeared to pick something up.

"My purse!" she exclaimed.

Before Indy could react, Boris and Dmitri came strolling up with elaborate casualness.

"Indy! Rosa!" said Boris. "What an amazing coincidence!"

"How was the concert?" asked Dmitri.

"It was canceled," said Rosa, rolling her eyes meaningfully at Dmitri and Boris. "I've been showing Indy the bridges of St. Petersburg for the last hour."

Boris was just as thoughtful and sensitive as ever.

"Poor devil!" he said. "The bridges of St. Petersburg are *so* boring."

Indy tried to look polite.

"Well, old fellow," said Boris, clapping an arm

around Indy's shoulder, "it's time to get you home, eh?"

"Yes," said Indy. He felt like exploding. "I was . . . just thinking the same thing."

Shortly after nine-thirty, Indy, Rosa, Boris, and Dmitri were climbing the stairs of their building. Indy pulled himself wearily up the last stretch. A dozen more steps and he could collapse in peace. He found the door and pulled it open.

"Surprise!" shouted a dozen voices. "Happy birthday, Indy!"

The room was packed with people: Sergei, Irina, regulars from the Bearpit café—everybody, it seemed, whom Indy had met since he'd arrived in Russia. Homemade decorations had been draped everywhere, and a large banner with Indy's name on it hung on the wall. The big table was covered with a makeshift birthday feast.

Indy stood there staring at it all for a moment—and then broke out into a huge grin. He'd forgotten all about his birthday. He was eighteen!

"Fooled you, huh?" said Irina, giving him a hug.

"But how did you know?" asked Indy.

"Your papers," said Rosa, putting her arm around him. "You left them here one day, and we couldn't help peeking."

"So that was why you were leading me all over St. Petersburg . . ." said Indy to Rosa, wagging a finger at her.

"Of course," said Boris. "We had to keep you out of the apartment *somehow*!"

Indy started to laugh.

Soon the party was in full swing. The concertinist from the Bearpit was playing and people were dancing wildly to old Russian folk tunes. Indy tried to join in. He crouched down with his arms folded and a Russian fur hat perched rakishly on his head. Just as he was about to fall over, Sergei rescued him.

"Hey, Indy! Quit showing off your fancy footwork and come and cut your cake! We're all hungry."

"A cake?" said Indy, astonished. He knew how short food was in the city.

"Certainly a cake," said Irina, stepping forward proudly with the flat, round loaf Indy had brought them earlier.

Now it was iced, with a single candle stuck in

the middle. Indy laughed as he recognized it.

"This is a revolutionary cake," Irina announced. "More ingenuity than raisins!"

Everyone applauded as Irina put the cake down on the table and Indy prepared to cut it. The whole party gathered around to watch. Boris, as usual, couldn't resist making a political joke.

"This is typical," he said jovially. "If there's a cake, who gets to divide it? The capitalist!"

They all laughed, including Indy, but Dmitri was worried he might be offended.

"Indy's not cutting the cake because he's a capitalist, Boris," he protested. "He's cutting it because it's his birthday."

Sergei couldn't resist joining in the joke, and he snatched the knife away from Indy.

"That's how things *used* to be, Dmitri. Everything used to depend on birth. Not just when you were born, but what sort of family you were born into!"

Irina promptly took the knife from Sergei and marked out a large slice.

"If you were born a noble—you got that much," she said. "But if you were born a peasant . . ."

"Or a worker . . ." added Sergei.

53

"You got that much," said Irina, marking out a very thin slice. "That was the way things were in Russia ever since the Middle Ages," she added contemptuously.

"And now the Czar's gone," said Sergei with satisfaction, "and we're through with it!"

"And a good thing, too," said Indy, grabbing the knife back. "Because now you have a chance to get rich—like in America. They're capitalists in America and not ashamed of it. Anybody who's smart enough can invent something, build a factory to make it, and sell it for as much money as he can get. Nobody'll try and stop him and nobody'll try to take the money away from him."

He pointed to the piece marked out by Irina for the aristocrats. "The guy who makes the cake gets that nice big slice!"

Sergei quickly whipped the knife out of Indy's hand. He was carried away with the argument now.

"And the workers who actually did the baking get little teeny bits! That's not fair!" he said. "So, the way to achieve justice is—"

Rosa decided to chime in. She took the knife and finished Sergei's sentence.

"The way to achieve justice is through socialism," she said. "Because then the capitalist is allowed to bake the cake but the government makes sure he divides it up fairly with the workers!"

She marked the icing up into a series of neat, equal portions.

"That won't work, Rosa," said Irina, shaking her head. "The capitalists are too smart for that. They'll always trick the people out of their fair share. The only solution is for the government to control everything—get all the ingredients for the cake together, build the cake factory, and divide it out fairly among *all* the people."

To prove her point, Irina cut the cake into equal slices along the lines marked out by Rosa.

"That's what Communism is all about!" she said.

"And this is anarchism in practice!" said Boris, grabbing several slices and cramming them into his mouth.

Indy laughed and bit into his cake. It tasted good, not because of what it was made of, who had baked it, or how much it cost—but because his friends had given it to him. Politics weren't what mattered. What counted was friendship. He raised his glass.

"To friendship!" Indy said.

And everyone answered his toast. "To friendship!"

Rosa gathered her courage and did something she'd been wanting to do for weeks. She kissed Indy's cheek.

"Because it's your birthday," she said as Indy looked at her in surprise.

"Thanks," he said, and blushed. Was Rosa getting a crush on him? No, he told himself. The idea was ridiculous. She was just being friendly.

"To our friend, Indy," said Irina, making a toast of her own.

There was more applause. Irina motioned for quiet.

"This is where if we were rich we'd give our friend a sumptuous present. But because we're not rich," continued Irina, "and in fact none of us has any money at all . . ."

"Hear! Hear!" shouted the others.

"We're going to give him something better. We're going to take him to see history being made!" said Irina.

There was a puzzled silence. Indy wondered what she had in mind.

"Come on, Indy," she said, taking his hand. "Let's go!"

In the basement of the French Embassy, Pierre Brossard (*center*) hands his analysis of the Bolshevik situation to Monsieur Laurentine while Indy struggles to prepare his own.

At the Bearpit Café, Indy shares bread from the embassy with his Russian friends (*left to right*) Sergei, Irina, Rosa, and Dmitri.

who can find out what the Bolsheviks are up to.

With Dmitri and Boris looking on, Indy beats Sergei in a game of chess in their apartment.

Irina gives Indy a birthday kiss.

At Indy's birthday party, Boris the anarchist *(right)* jokingly objects to a capitalist cutting the cake.

Irina urges the Putilov steelworkers to revolt against the Provisional Government.

Lenin stirs up his Bolshevik followers at the Keshinskiya Mansion.

Despite machine gunners on the rooftops, Indy leads Rosa across the street toward the doomed procession of steelworkers.

The massacre begins. Indy (*left, in hat*) rushes to protect Irina as she tries to reach the wounded Sergei.

Chapter 6

The Keshinskiya Mansion had once belonged to a beautiful ballet dancer. She had been a favorite of the Czar's. The mansion had huge bedrooms, elegant suites, balconies overlooking the garden, and a great ballroom. Before the revolution, Keshinskiya was the scene of magnificent parties. Dancers, actors, painters, playwrights, nobles, bankers—the cream of Old Russia—had filled the house . . . laughing and chattering, sipping fine wines, delicately nibbling caviar, dancing to the music of orchestras.

No more. The ballerina had fled. Keshinskiya was the headquarters of the most determined band of revolutionaries the world had ever seen—the Bolsheviks.

Under the Czar, the Bolsheviks had gone into exile all over Europe and beyond to avoid prison or death. As soon as the Czar fell, they began to pour back into Russia. The returning Bolsheviks were grim-faced idealists in baggy, uncared-for clothes. They intended to rebuild Russia according to the theories of one man— a white-bearded German economist named Karl Marx.

Indy and his friends entered the tall foyer of the Keshinskiya Mansion. Liveried footmen had once taken the top hats and evening cloaks of dukes and counts in that same foyer. Now hundreds of ordinary people in threadbare clothes were pushing and jostling for a chance to get into the ballroom. They wanted to hear the man who was going to turn Karl Marx's ideas into reality—the Bolshevik leader Vladimir Ilyich Lenin. Lenin was determined to make Russia the world's first Communist state.

"When you hear Lenin speak, Indy," said Sergei, beaming with pride, "*then* you'll know what Communism is all about."

Sergei took his friend by the arm and hauled him through the throng. Indy gasped at the superb room the Bolsheviks had taken over. Golden pillars rose along the walls and sparkling chandeliers hung from the ceiling. Their crystals reflected light onto the eager faces of men and women who would never have been allowed to set foot here in the old days.

As Lenin stepped onto the platform, cheers echoed through the room and shook the chandeliers till they tinkled.

Vladimir Ilyich Lenin would never have become a great leader if looks had been important. He was a short, squat man with a bald head and eyes that looked as if they had been pulled up at the corners. Nor was he a speaker who could hold a crowd with the sheer beauty of his voice or the elegance of his words.

But Lenin could hold people spellbound because he was a man of enormous force—immensely intelligent and fantastically determined. Watching him, Indy remembered that Lenin's older brother, Alexander, had been hanged when he was just seventeen—almost Indy's age—for trying to assassinate the Czar. Lenin was only twelve at the time. Perhaps that memory had helped him to endure years of poverty and exile, patiently waiting for the day when he would get the chance to change Russia.

When the Czar had fallen last February, Lenin had been in Switzerland. All Germany lay between him and home. He was almost mad with frustration. The revolution for which he had worked for so many years was happening without him! Against all odds, he persuaded the Germans to let him cross their territory in a sealed train. It was sealed so that Lenin couldn't try to persuade German workers to revolt, too.

He'd arrived at the Finland Station in St. Petersburg in April. Crowds of Russian workers gave him an ecstatic welcome. Ever since then Lenin had been firing them up with his ideas for a new Russia. They could make it happen themselves, if only they were bold enough.

"Comrades!" said Lenin as he stuck his hands in his waistcoat pockets. "A question: How many more of our young men have to die in this war before the capitalists who started it are satisfied? Before they have made enough money out of it?"

There was an answering buzz of agreement from the packed room. Nearly everyone had relatives at the front. Many had been there themselves. Most of them had little idea of why the Czar had gotten Russia involved in the war in the first place. Very few of them understood why Kerensky and the Provisional Government were insisting Russia had to continue fighting. Kerensky said that Russia had to honor her promise to help her allies, France and Britain, defeat the Germans. The new Russia had to be dependable. But Lenin was telling them that that was rubbish. All the war was really about was profit.

"Who profits from the guns and shells and bombs that explode every day all over Europe?" he demanded. "The soldiers who fire them? Of course not! It is the capitalists who manufacture them and sell them to governments! That is what this war is about—how much money those capitalists can make before it's all over!"

The crowd murmured angrily. They'd seen those rich, well-fed people riding through the streets in their carriages. Meanwhile workers slept on factory floors because they couldn't even afford a room. And now they were supposed to go on fighting a war so the rich could go on making money!

"How many more must be killed before they

have enough?" repeated Lenin. "Ten thousand? Fifty thousand? A million? Two million?" His voice thundered through the room like cannon fire. "I say—NONE! I say—stop the war NOW!"

The entire room erupted in cheers. Even Indy found it hard not to join in. He'd seen the horrors of this war—the endless mud and blood, the months-long battles over a few hundred yards of ruined earth. What *was* the point of it?

Lenin plunged on. "Our demands are simple," he said. "We want peace for our soldiers. We want bread for the workers. We want land for our peasants! And we want them NOW!"

A swell of cheers built through the room. Lenin raised a hand to still the crowd.

"But that's only the beginning," said Lenin. "When we come to power we will *utterly change* this nation into something the world has never seen before! Under Communism, Russia will be governed by the people in one great armed militia. Ordinary people will run their everyday affairs *themselves!* We will have a state ruled by ordinary workers—the dictatorship of the proletariat!"

Another swell of cheers filled the room, slowly

quieting as Lenin continued in a different tone. It seemed to Indy that Lenin had a heroic vision of a country more kind and just than the world had ever seen.

"And one day, I predict," he said, "Russia will develop into a society so perfect that the state itself will wither away. There will be no need for police, or armies, or government bureaucrats! Everyone will share with everyone else. People will work together in freedom. There will be no rich, no poor, no oppressors, and no oppressed. Just—harmony. That is what Communism is all about."

Indy was impressed. It sounded wonderful!

"What do Kerensky and the Provisional Government offer instead?" Lenin paused for a moment to let his audience think. "Capitalism—with *lighter chains* for the workers! There can be no compromise with these frauds!

"That," said Lenin, "is the message we must hammer home in every factory, barracks, and village in Russia. Peace! Bread! Land! Keep on saying it until all Russia rises up to demand it. And then—*then*—we will lead the proletariat to victory!"

The cheering reached a new pitch. Dozens of

people threw their hats into the air in exultation. Several hats hung from the ballerina's chandeliers like trophies.

"Well, Indy," said Irina, hugging him. "Happy birthday!"

And Indy hugged her back. She was right. This *was* history, happening right before his eyes. He was certain that Lenin was going to change the world. For good or ill—it was too soon to say.

As the crowd began to surge out of the ballroom, Indy couldn't see Sergei anywhere. Then he noticed him arguing with a man in a black cap. It was hard to hear what they were saying above the din. But the occasional word came across.

"Not yet, I tell you!" insisted the man in the black cap. "He said so!"

Indy wondered who said what. It sounded important, so he kept his ears open.

"He's wrong!" said Sergei, clearly very agitated. "The soldiers are falling back on the battlefront! Now is the time!"

But the other man was unconvinced.

"No! The timing is—" Indy couldn't hear the next word. Then the man said, "Get it wrong now and it all goes up in smoke!"

Just as Indy began to realize he was on to something, he felt a hand on his arm.

"Come on, Indy," said Irina. "Let's get out of this crowd."

"Right," he said. "I need to get home and get some sleep. But thanks. This is about the most interesting birthday I ever had."

But as the crowd swirled them out into the night, Indy had something besides sleep on his mind. How could he make use of what he'd just overheard? Could Sergei's words free him from that basement office?

Chapter 7

Indy had a knack of fixing a time in his head and waking up when that hour came around. So though he fell asleep as soon as his head touched the pillow, at two-thirty A.M. his eyes promptly blinked open.

After just a few hours' sleep, going out again was the last thing Indy wanted to do. But after hearing Lenin's speech and Sergei's conversation, he knew he didn't have much time. The Bolsheviks were about ready for action. To find out what he needed to know, he'd have to take some risks. Right now.

Silently, Indy slipped on his clothes and made his way on stocking feet to the door. He couldn't afford to wake any of his roommates. Soundlessly, he turned the door handle. Then he crept down the stairs and sat on the steps outside to put on his boots. Five minutes later he'd been swallowed up by the night.

The street seemed completely empty. No lights showed in any of the windows and no sound came from any of the buildings. It was not surprising. Most of them were little machine outfits—metalworking shops, small factories—deserted at night by their weary workers. Indy slipped along under the cover of the overhanging eaves.

Then he stopped and peered around him. There it was—the People's Printing Works. The name was painted in badly lettered red characters above the front door.

Taking no notice of the front door, Indy crept past the building to a narrow alley between the factories. He glanced in both directions along the street. Convinced he wasn't being followed, he disappeared up the dark alley. Then he clambered over another wall into a rubbish-strewn yard at the back of the People's Printing Works.

Glass crunched as he dropped to the ground. He shrank back against the wall, but none of the black shapes in the yard moved. Stepping gingerly through the debris, Indy made his way to the back wall of the printing works. He followed the brickwork until he finally came to a window—and silently groaned. The window was barred from top to bottom!

Indy had come too far to be put off by an obstacle like this. Taking out his bowie knife, he jammed it as hard as he could between the bricks into which the bars were bolted. He was worried the knife might snap off and break. But to his delight, the mortar gave way easily. He grinned to himself.

Using the knife as a lever, he pried out the first brick. The second was easy. Within minutes Indy was able to lift out not just the iron bars, but the window itself. He hauled himself up to what remained of the sill and dropped silently to the floor inside.

Indy froze. What if there were guard dogs? They'd tear out his throat! But guard dogs would have started barking by now. There was no one in the People's Printing Works but Indiana Jones!

Indy was pleased with the reasoning that had brought him here. If the Bolsheviks wanted to start an uprising by putting tens of thousands of people on the streets, they'd have to distribute tens of thousands of leaflets with dates, times, and places. All the leaflets he'd collected so far suggested things were building steadily. But obviously the Bolsheviks weren't going to let anyone know the crucial facts until the last minute.

On the other hand, they'd have to be ready. The printing plant was the logical place to find leaflets with the information he needed.

Indy reached into his pocket, drew out a packet of matches, and lit a stub of candle. He knew any light was dangerous, but he had no choice. Huge, sinister-looking printing presses loomed up in the darkness. Piles of leaflets and posters were stacked on tables next to them.

Forcing himself not to hurry, Indy methodically went from pile to pile, looking carefully to see if any of them was the kind of thing he was looking for. Most of the papers were just routine—party membership cards, general propaganda about peace, bread, and land. He pocketed anything that looked even halfway interesting. And then he picked up a leaflet that made him catch his breath.

"Workers and peasants," he translated the Russian words to himself. "The moment has come for the people to strike without mercy and bring Kerensky and his henchmen down into the dust of history. We will gather on _____ and march on the Tauride Palace at _____."

The date and time had been left blank! It was obviously an unfinished proof of the leaflet he wanted. But was there a finished version? One that gave the exact time and date of the Bolshevik uprising? He had to find out.

He continued going through the piles of papers stacked on tables next to the presses. His fingers grew black from the printer's ink. Somewhere among the scores of piles lay his prize. He was certain of it! He put the candle down on a press and began to go through the piles with both hands.

Suddenly the front door of the printing plant opened with a loud bang. Indy's heart leaped right up into his throat. He pinched out the flame of the candle just as the door slammed back against the wall and the light went on.

Two men carrying rifles came into the room. Indy couldn't see them—printing presses were in the way—but he could hear them clearly. Particularly the solid clunk of their rifle bolts as they unslung them from their shoulders.

"See!" said the first man. "I told you there's nobody here."

Indy slid under one of the presses and tried to draw his legs out of sight. But there wasn't quite enough room.

"I'm certain I saw a light in here, comrade," the second man said.

"Imagination," said the first stolidly. But as he walked down the aisle between the wall and the machines, he saw Indy's candle on the press. "Look at this!" he said. "The wax is still warm. Someone's here! You take that side. I'll take this one. And fire the moment you see *anything*."

Indy's feet still stuck out of his hiding place beneath the press like two signs saying, "Come and get me!" But as he tried to scrunch himself up, his elbow accidentally hit a button on the press. The machine made a clunking noise and started spewing out new leaflets.

The Bolsheviks leaped toward the sound and started shooting. At the same instant Indy bolted out of his hiding place and ran for the rear wall.

The two men hurled themselves after him. Bullets ricocheted off the machinery. Indy sprinted desperately for the window. At last he reached it and, with an incredible leap, tumbled out into the night.

But there was no stopping. The two Bolsheviks were chasing right after him, down the alley and through the empty streets. Their gunfire echoed off the old stones. Their bullets blasted chunks of masonry and sprays of brick dust from the walls.

Then Indy felt a sharp, stinging pain in his neck. He'd been hit! But he kept on running. When he put his hand up to his neck, he realized that he had only felt a piece of flying stone. A near miss.

He pounded over one of the humpbacked bridges. Thanks to Rosa's lesson in St. Petersburg geography, now he knew just where to go. A bullet sang past his head. He dived to the right and headed down a long, straight road to the embassy square.

He knew he was a perfect target. There were no convenient shadows here to mask his movements. He heard the two men clatter around the corner, heard the sound of their rifle fire.

He focused on the embassy. Reach it! Reach

it! Reach it! His legs seemed to take on a life of their own. Reach it! A sharp outcrop of bricks scraped against his shoulder, but he didn't feel them. At last the tree-lined embassy square lay silent before him. He was there!

Gasping for breath, he ran up to the great iron gate and hauled on the bell again and again. Finally a light went on in the embassy. Behind him, he could hear the Bolsheviks shouting as they ran toward the square. He hauled on the bell again.

Slowly, painfully slowly, the great door of the embassy opened and the duty officer peered out uncertainly.

"Quick! It's me—Captain Défense!" shouted Indy.

The duty officer came down to the gate and looked at him.

"What is it?" he said.

"OPEN THE GATE!" yelled Indy.

Finally the duty officer opened the gate, just as the Bolsheviks burst into the square. Indy dived right past the officer, up the steps of the embassy, and through the door. He slid helplessly across the marble floor of the foyer, with leaflets dropping out of his pockets in all directions. He'd made it!

Chapter 8

The duty officer insisted on making a report in his logbook about Indy's unconventional arrival. Watching how slowly the guy dotted each *i*, Indy felt lucky to be alive to sign the report. Another thirty seconds at the gate and he might have been blown to kingdom come.

Finally the duty officer, satisfied that the formalities had been completed, shuffled back to his cubbyhole. Indy gathered up his scattered sheets and hurried downstairs to his own little cubbyhole—and stopped.

A light was shining under the door. Someone was in there. Someone who'd gotten past the duty officer. Someone who knew where he'd been that night. Someone who was waiting for him. . . .

Indy shoved the leaflets in his pockets, crept up to the door, and crouched down below the doorknob. Reaching up gingerly, he turned the knob a fraction of an inch at a time. Then he ripped the door open and flung himself at floor level into the room.

Pierre Brossard looked down at him from the far side of the table and smiled politely.

"Ah, Captain. How nice of you to drop in."

"Don't you *ever* go home?" asked Indy.

Feeling like an absolute fool, Indy got to his feet and dusted himself off. Brossard watched him curiously for a moment and then turned back to his papers. His side of the desk was a solid mass of documents, handwritten notes, typed lists.

Indy casually shoved his hands into his pockets, acting as if sliding into rooms on his stomach was his favorite method of arriving anywhere. He stalked around behind Brossard's chair and looked over his shoulder.

Brossard immediately covered the papers in

front of him, like a kid in an exam who doesn't want another kid to see his answers.

Just to annoy him, Indy repeated the only words he'd been able to see before Brossard had hidden them.

"The Putilov Steelworks, eh?" Indy asked, sitting at his own side of the desk. "That's your best deduction so far?"

He'd no idea whether the Putilov Steelworks was important or not. He just wanted Brossard to think he was ahead of him. But his words stung his rival to the core.

"It's only the key to the whole thing!" said Brossard.

Indy was now intrigued. Perhaps he *ought* to know about the Putilov Steelworks.

"Come on!" Indy said, fishing by provoking Brossard. "The Putilov Steelworks is just another big industrial plant. It doesn't mean anything."

"Défense," said Brossard angrily, "it's the biggest concentration of industrial workers in St. Petersburg. It's the litmus paper for the whole city. When those people are ready to attack the government, the Bolsheviks will strike."

"I'll remember that," said Indy smugly.

Brossard realized Indy had tricked him into saying more than he should have. He returned, scowling, to his papers. Indy put his feet on his desk and started pulling leaflets out of his pockets and making more notes on his now much-scribbled-on calendar.

It was dawn when Indy got back home. Once again he crept up the stairs, exhausted. He'd taken the notes from the office with him. He wasn't going to risk Brossard's looking over his calculations. His calendar was tucked under his arm.

Then he turned the corner into his corridor and stopped dead. A dark figure was silhouetted against the window at the far end, waiting for him. For a moment they stared at each other without moving.

"Hi, Indy," said Rosa.

Indy's relief turned to puzzlement as he sat down on a window seat next to her.

"Rosa," said Indy softly. "Have you been waiting here . . ."

His voice petered out as he realized that Rosa had been waiting for *him*. And that it had nothing to do with the Bolsheviks.

"Just since the party," she said. Rosa looked at him for a long time before she could bring herself to speak.

"I just wanted to tell you," she got out at last. "I just wanted to tell you—I love you."

Indy didn't know what to say. He liked Rosa a lot. But love? No!

Rosa understood his silence.

"I shouldn't be saying this, should I?" she said. "I'm embarrassing you."

"No—it's just—" mumbled Indy.

But Rosa, now that she had decided to admit her feelings, had to continue.

"Indy," she said, "when I'm with you, I feel— alive. When you're gone, it's as if somebody's just shut me in a tomb."

"Rosa—" began Indy, searching for the right words.

"It's okay, Indy," said Rosa gently. "You don't need to say anything. I got it wrong, didn't I?"

"Rosa, I like you so much," he said. "You're funny, and smart, and pretty. But love is a weird thing. It strikes like lightning and you can't make it strike, any more than you can stop it if it decides to hit you."

"And you haven't been struck," said Rosa.

In reply, Indy reached out and took her hand

sympathetically. Rosa's eyes glistened and tears began slowly rolling down her cheeks.

"I sometimes envy Sergei and Irina," she said. "They've got it all planned out, you know. As soon as the revolution is over they're going to move out into the country and just forget about the rest of the world."

"Yeah, I know," said Indy. "Sergei's going to build a log cabin by a stream and catch fish. They're going to have two cats and four dogs and seven children."

"I sometimes think when they're telling the steelworkers to storm the barricades all they're really thinking about is that little cabin in the country," Rosa said with a sigh.

"The steelworkers?" he said suddenly, staring at Rosa.

"Oh, I meant any workers," said Rosa. "I just said that because they're going to talk to some steelworkers this morning."

"Which steelworkers?" asked Indy, gripping her hand. "Did they say *which* steel plant they were going to?"

"Oh, Indy, I don't know. What does it matter?" Rosa looked at him, puzzled by his sudden change of mood.

Just then Sergei and Irina came out, carrying

their red banner. They stopped in surprise when they saw Indy and Rosa.

"Hi!" said Sergei. "Are we interrupting something?"

"Sergei, you are so *dumb* sometimes," said Irina. She took him by the arm and began pulling him away down the hall. "See you later, kids," she said.

"Good luck at the Putilov Works!" Indy called after them.

They stopped in their tracks, and Sergei turned around.

"What makes you think we're going there?" he demanded.

"You'll have to whip up the Putilov workers if the revolution's starting tomorrow, won't you?" Indy said, using Brossard's logic.

"What are you talking about, Indy?" said Irina.

Indy pulled a handful of leaflets out of his pocket.

"I've been reading the literature, Irina," he said. "All the fliers about rallies and meetings and marches. I know they're happening all the time." He took out the calendar with its circled dates and waved it at them. "But there's more of them happening in the next forty-eight hours than there have been for weeks. I've even seen fliers that haven't been printed yet! I know the Putilov Steelworks is the key. And now I know you're on your way to stir them up. So don't tell me the Bolshevik Revolution isn't starting now, Sergei."

Irina and Sergei looked at each other, alarmed. Then Sergei put down the banner.

"You've got to find this out to tell your spy bosses, haven't you, Indy?" he said. "That's okay, I understand. Everybody has a job to do. Well, let me do you a favor. Don't tell them the Bolsheviks are making their move now, because they aren't."

"Well, you would say that, wouldn't you?" retorted Indy icily. "You've got to—"

Sergei put a hand on Indy's shoulder.

"The first thing is that we're not going to the Putilov Steelworks," he said firmly. "We're going to a steelworks, but not that one. That doesn't matter, but I'm going to tell you something that does. Indy, where do you think Lenin is?"

"As of last night he was at Bolshevik Head-quarters," said Indy, "where he probably is—"

"He's on his way to Finland," interrupted Sergei.

"Finland?" said Indy, unable to believe his ears. Finland was only a few hours away by train, but surely—another *country?*

"The man is exhausted, Indy," said Sergei. "He's worn out and he's gone to recuperate. Now ask yourself this—have you ever heard of a revolution starting when the leader was on vacation?"

"But that's not the reason the Bolsheviks aren't making their move now," Irina said. "It's much more basic than that. Russia isn't ready."

"Lenin knows we could take St. Petersburg right now," said Sergei.

"And hold it for about week—no more— before we got thrown out," added Irina.

"The simple fact is that not enough people support us yet," said Sergei. "Not enough soldiers, not enough workers, not enough peasants. We'd be wiped out."

"In a few months' time we'll have the people on our side," said Irina. "Not just the people in the city, but people all over Russia. Then will be the time to do something bold—not now."

Indy looked from one to the other. Were they telling the truth?

"If you go and tell your bosses the Bolshevik

Revolution is coming anytime soon," Sergei said, "you'll end up looking pretty silly, I promise you. Believe me, Indy, this is not the time."

Irina took Sergei by the hand. Sergei picked up the banner.

"See you later, Indy," he said.

As Indy watched them walk away, he felt Rosa staring at him. He had completely forgotten her.

There was a strange expression on her face, as if she was seeing him for the first time.

"Friendship isn't easy either, is it, Indy?" she said.

Chapter 9

It was four hours later on the morning of the same day. Indy had caught a couple of hours' sleep, cleaned himself up, and managed to get to work on time. Just. Infuriatingly, Brossard, who had probably not left the office all night, looked as immaculate as if he had spent the night in a first-class hotel.

Now both Indy and Brossard were in the Ambassador's big conference room. They sat around the gleaming, waxed table with all the top brass of the embassy. The Ambassador was striding up and down, talking to them urgently.

"I need results now! The pressure for information is not merely from the Russian government but, far more important, from my superiors in Paris. They're demanding a report today on a possible Bolshevik uprising. Your assessments?"

Everyone glanced uneasily at each other. Then Indy decided boldness was his best course.

"Sir—!" he said, about to launch into his speech.

But at precisely the same instant, Brossard made a statement so dramatic that everyone turned right to him.

"I believe the Bolshevik uprising will begin within the next twenty-four hours, Ambassador," he said.

The Ambassador stopped pacing.

"Really, Captain Brossard?" he said. "What's your proof?"

Brossard, of course, was perfectly prepared. He laid out a sheet of paper on the table and began listing the points he'd noted.

"Proof one, sir," Brossard said, "comes from the battlefront. The latest Russian attack against the Germans is failing. More and more soldiers are deserting from the front."

"What does that mean?" Indy interrupted.

But nobody was listening to him.

"Proof two," Brossard went on, "is that regiments stationed in St. Petersburg itself are refusing to go to the front at all. That means they're available for an uprising here. The most dangerous are the Machine Gun Regiment and the Kronstadt sailors."

"However—" said Indy, but Brossard went on like a bulldozer.

"Proof three: In the next forty-eight hours there are more rallies and protest meetings scheduled than at any time since the Czar fell."

Indy ground his teeth. That was *his* idea. How could Brossard have thought of it, too?

"I believe these events are about to culminate in a march on the Tauride Palace within twenty-four hours," concluded Brossard smoothly.

Worried faces stared at each other all around the table. The Ambassador looked at the neat young man in spectacles, impressed.

"Cogent reasoning, Brossard," he said. "What is your view, André?"

"Well," said the First Secretary thoughtfully,

"if the Bolsheviks storm the Palace now, there'll be precious little to stop them. Very few troops are available to defend the Provisional Government. Loyal units could be rushed back to St. Petersburg from the front, but it would take days."

A gloomy silence fell on the room. It was now or never for Indy to make his case and put Brossard in his place.

"Except for the fact that the timing is entirely wrong," Indy said quietly.

"Wrong, Captain Défense? Why wrong?" asked the Ambassador

Suddenly everyone was listening to him. No one even greeted Monsieur Laurentine, who rushed in late, carrying some files.

"Because the Bolsheviks haven't got enough support in either the country or the army yet, sir," Indy said, remembering what Sergei had said almost word for word. "They know they could capture St. Petersburg in a couple of days, but they also know they couldn't hold it. They're not going to strike till they're sure they have enough support from people throughout the country."

"There's a lot of truth in that, Ambassador," said the First Secretary. "The Bolsheviks are dangerous, but they're also cautious. Most of their leaders have spent years in exile, preparing for a chance like this. Lenin was in Switzerland. Leon Trotsky just came back from New York City. They're not going to ruin it by attacking before they're certain they can win."

"What's more," said Indy, following up his advantage, "I've been among the Bolshevik activists—the ones who'd *have* to know if anything was going on. And they know nothing."

"It's Bolshevik practice to keep ordinary members in the dark," said Brossard contemptuously. "Everything Lenin said has been firing them up to—"

But this time Indy rode right over him.

"Brossard may be totally wrong in most of his analysis," Indy said sweetly, twisting the knife. "But he is right to mention Lenin. If you want to know what's going on in this revolution, follow Lenin."

"Well, naturally we do follow Lenin, Captain Défense," said the Ambassador confidently. "We have agents who do nothing else."

"Then I suggest you check with them right now, Ambassador," said Indy. "I think you'll find that as of last night he's on vacation in

Finland. Hardly the right place from which to mount a revolution in St. Petersburg."

Indy's words hit like a bombshell. How was this young man so certain about the whereabouts of one of the most secretive men in Russia? Even Brossard looked impressed. In fact, Indy was quaking inside. He only had Sergei's word that Lenin was in Finland. What if Sergei was wrong?

"Monsieur Laurentine," said the Ambassador. "Do we have those reports?"

Laurentine opened a file he'd been given.

"The reports have just arrived, sir," he said crisply, scanning them as he spoke. He gave Indy a startled look and turned to the Ambassador. "Captain Défense is quite correct, Ambassador," he announced. "Lenin crossed the Finnish border this morning. He's reported to be suffering from extreme nervous exhaustion."

There were murmurs all around the room. Indy closed his eyes and heaved a silent sigh of relief.

"Hah!" said the First Secretary.

"Indeed?" said the Ambassador. "Well done, Défense. Good intelligence work. You may have a future out in the field.

"Interesting thinking, Brossard," he added with a slightly patronizing edge to his voice. "But perhaps you let your enthusiasm run away with you.

"Thank you, gentlemen," he said, taking the file from Laurentine. "I think I have what I need to report to Paris. I'll study the documents, but I'm pleased to say it looks as though the second Russian Revolution is not upon us—yet."

The Ambassador walked briskly out, a man with a weight lifted from his shoulders.

"Better luck next time," said Indy to Brossard smugly.

Chapter 10

In his basement cubbyhole, Indy finished decoding the last message and glanced at his watch. The working day was over, he was pleased to see. He was looking forward to a long, quiet evening with his friends. He'd give them hints, perhaps, of the great impression he'd made on his bosses with his performance that morning.

Brossard was hunched over his desk, shifting papers from file to file. He and Indy had scarcely exchanged a word since they'd walked out of the Ambassador's room that morning. Brossard still felt hot with fury and embarrassment.

"Okay, I think that's it for today," said Indy, getting up and stretching. Part of him felt sorry for his humiliated colleague, but somehow he couldn't resist a few gloating words before he left.

"I'm telling you, I'm glad I'm not going to be doing this for much longer. You're a good deskman, Brossard. But I need to be out in the real world."

"Is that so, Captain?" said Brossard, still shuffling papers.

"See, I like *doing* things," Indy said expansively. "Not just reading about them, like you. And, well—I believe it's going to pay off. I'll think of you, Pierre, plugging away down here while I'm out tracking the enemy through the streets of some exotic city."

"Good," said Brossard expressionlessly. "It's nice to know someone cares about you."

Indy wasn't quite sure how to respond to that remark. But he didn't have to. The door suddenly burst open and slammed against the wall. Indy stepped back in alarm as Monsieur Laurentine appeared in the room like a small, plump tornado. His eyes glistened with some strong emotion Indy didn't immediately recognize.

"Captain Défense, Captain Brossard—report at once to the crisis room above the Ambassador's office," he said tightly.

"The crisis room?" said Indy. "I didn't know we had—"

"We didn't," replied Laurentine grimly. "We've just opened one. You see, the Bolshevik uprising began an hour ago."

Monsieur Laurentine turned on his heel and marched out, leaving Indy looking like a man who had just been hit on the head by a large pole.

Indy felt sick as he mounted the great marble stairs behind a smug, smiling Brossard. He felt sicker still as he walked in on a scene of intense, almost frantic activity in the room above the Ambassador's office. Every diplomat, servant, and secretary in the embassy seemed to be there. A flock of people were carrying in typewriters, setting up tables, fixing maps of St. Petersburg and Russia to the wall, and hurrying to and fro with dispatches and documents. A row of telephones rang constantly.

"Ah! Out of your basement, Captain," the Ambassador said, eyeing Indy coldly.

"I'd like you to man one of the phones, Défense," said Monsieur Laurentine. "Brossard, over here with me."

The First Secretary hurried to the Ambassador.

"The Machine Gun Regiment has taken over the Finland railroad station, Ambassador," he said.

"They're going around to all the army units stationed in the city, urging them to join in overthrowing the government," added the Second Secretary.

The Ambassador gave Indy a look that would have cut through metal. But he took out his anger on the Second Secretary.

"Mark it on the map, man," he snarled. "Mark it on the map. I want to *see* what's going on."

The Second Secretary hurried over to the St. Petersburg map and shifted a flag marked with the insignia of the regiment.

Indy hid himself in the line of telephone answerers. He was so humiliated he could hardly think straight.

Just hours ago he had shown he was an intelligence man to be reckoned with. A spy with

contacts, the ability to put facts together, boldness. Now he was a blundering fool. Worse—a
blundering fool who made the French Ambassador look like a fool to *his* bosses in Paris.
Brossard had had the right information. And he,
Indiana Jones, had made sure that it was ig-
nored! And all because he'd been taken in by
those two lying, scheming Bolsheviks! Sergei
and Irena, pretending to be his friends and
leading him step by step down the garden path.
Lousy rotten traitors!

The phone rang and he picked it up, then
wrote down the message mechanically.

"At the intersection of where?" he said dully.
"Liteiny Street and the Nevsky Prospect. Right.
Thanks."

He filled in the message form and took it to
Monsieur Laurentine.

"There are Bolshevik armored cars at the
intersection of Liteiny Street and the Nevsky
Prospect, sir," he said.

"There are Bolshevik armored cars at *all* the
major intersections, Captain. Thank you," said
Laurentine brusquely. "I think your phone is
ringing again."

"They're blocking bridges over the Neva, sir,"
reported another telephone answerer.

"Very well," said Laurentine. "I'll have it marked on the map."

The Ambassador was standing in front of the city map. He watched grimly as the number of red flags multiplied steadily, moving nearer and nearer the center. The First Secretary came up to him with a new report and spoke confidentially in his ear.

"Lenin has returned from Finland, Your Excellency," whispered the First Secretary. "He's gone straight to Bolshevik Headquarters at the Keshinskiya Mansion and is addressing a massive crowd."

The Ambassador looked at him expressionlessly. It was just as he feared. With every piece of news he could feel his own standing in the espionage service crumble about him. And all because of that *stupid*, overconfident young man!

"The Kronstadt sailors are heading for the capital," said the Second Secretary as he added another flag to the map. "Five thousand of them."

"Wonderful," said the Ambassador sarcastically.

Brossard bustled up, doing his best to conceal his glee at the way things were turning out.

"Trotsky is addressing a giant crowd outside the Tauride Palace," said Brossard. "The mob is demanding the overthrow of the Provisional Government. Kerensky is away at the front, but other ministers are inside the Palace. There are virtually no troops to defend them."

"Quite," said the Ambassador.

Indy handed a message to Monsieur Laurentine but no one spoke to Captain Défense. He went back to his phone as quickly as possible. It was ringing insistently again.

"Yes?" said Indy. "The Putilov Steelworks? Okay."

He started filling out the message form. "Whipping up the workers? Okay. Persuading them to march on the capital? Right. Any names? Sergei Aliev . . . and Irina Michailovna Bochareva, right?" Indy added before the caller gave him her name. "Oh, I just guessed. That's all."

He hung up and stared despondently at his note. It was no more than he'd expected, but it still made him feel worse than ever. His so-called friends had even deceived him about which steelworks they were going to.

"The liars," he said to himself. "Dirty Red liars."

Indy turned to the telephone answerer next to him and spoke bitterly, not expecting a reply.

"If there's one thing you learn in a revolution," he said, "it's never to trust anybody who says he's your friend."

An hour later the Ambassador was still watching the red flags steadily fill the map. His lukewarm coffee somehow only served to make him feel more weary. The First Secretary came and sat beside him, less because he had anything to say than because the Ambassador looked so downcast.

"Well, sir, it looks as though a few hours from now you could be the first French ambassador to Bolshevik Russia," he said, trying to put a cheerful gloss on the situation.

The Ambassador looked at him dolefully.

"A few hours from now, André, I won't be an ambassador at all. France will never recognize a Russia run by the Communists."

Monsieur Laurentine joined them, perching on the edge of a chair next to the Ambassador's. He was strangely excited.

"I have the text of Lenin's speech to the Kronstadt sailors, sir. It's just come in."

The Ambassador looked at him without interest.

"Don't bother to read it, Laurentine. I know what it says. 'All power to the people. Forward to the Tauride Palace.' "

"Well, not exactly, Ambassador," said Monsieur Laurentine. "Let me read his actual words:

" 'Comrades—you must excuse me. I have been ill. In spite of temporary difficulties, I am certain we will be victorious, although this demands from us restraint, determination, and constant alertness.' "

"That's not exactly fighting talk," said the First Secretary.

"We also know now what Trotsky was telling the crowds at the Tauride Palace," said Laurentine, fishing out another message form.

"Which was?" said the Ambassador.

"Go home," said Laurentine simply.

"Go home?" repeated the Ambassador, hardly able to believe his ears.

Laurentine read from his notes: " 'The time is not right for an uprising. Disperse until you are called on.' "

Suddenly the clues began to fall together into a pattern. By chance the Ambassador's eye fell on Indy, still at his phone. Had that young man been right after all? Was it possible that Lenin had been called back to the capital only because events had taken a course none of the Bolsheviks expected?

"Good heavens," said the Ambassador.

"Perhaps Lenin really was on vacation. Perhaps it wasn't a ruse."

"Are people listening to these instructions to go home?" asked the First Secretary sharply.

Brossard bustled up again, waving a clutch of papers, and answered the question for him.

"No, sir," he said. "I have reports here from all over the city. The Bolshevik leaders are trying to restrain the people. But nobody's taking any notice. Processions are heading for the Tauride Palace from every direction. It's chaos."

"I'm beginning to like the sound of this," said the Ambassador. He suddenly looked his usual animated self. "It has the smell of disaster about it."

"The Cossacks are out, sir," reported Indy directly to the Ambassador. "They've decided to back the government. There are snipers on the rooftops firing on the marchers."

"That, Captain, is the sort of news I like to hear," said the Ambassador with a gleam in his eye. "Bloodshed, eh?"

"Yes, sir," said Indy. Since the early days of the czars, the fierce Cossack troops could always be counted on for a tough fight.

"You know what's happened, don't you?" The Ambassador grinned wolfishly. "You and Brossard were *both* right. The uprising *was* going to begin within twenty-four hours, as Brossard said. But the Bolshevik leadership didn't intend it to happen, as *you* said. They knew it was the wrong time.

"Our friend Lenin has overexcited the people. They've listened to one speech too many and they've taken the initiative themselves. Now the people are dragging Lenin, Trotsky, and their friends behind them. And the consequence will be—a Bolshevik rout," he said dramatically.

"By tomorrow morning," predicted Monsieur Laurentine, almost smacking his lips, "the streets of St. Petersburg will be running with blood."

"And *all* of it Red!" added the Ambassador.

The little group around him laughed, and Indy's stomach turned. He went back to his telephone.

"I took this for you while you were gone," said the girl next to him. "The Bolsheviks at the Putilov Steelworks are getting ready to lead thirty thousand men, women, and children in a march on the Palace. And you know what? They're going to run right into a barrage of Cossack machine guns."

Indy looked at her blankly. "What?"

The girl pointed to the map.

"The Cossacks are waiting for them, right across their route, ready to fire. They won't know what hit them, Captain."

Indy's brain began to function again, and he could vividly picture exactly what she was talking about. Too vividly.

"I've got to go out now," he said.

"But, Captain, your phone is ringing," said the girl.

"Let it," said Indy.

He left the crisis room without looking back. He had his own crisis to deal with now.

Chapter 11

The Putilov Steelworks, on the outskirts of St. Petersburg, was a vast, grim fortress of capitalism. Its blackened chimneys belched smoke into the sky. Its maze of smelters, blast furnaces, and rolling mills covered acre after acre.

Ignoring the curious glances of the workers, Indy hurried through the complex. He asked again and again if anyone had seen a young revolutionary named Irina and her companion, Sergei. At last someone directed him to a long, ramshackle building where the workers ate.

Indy pushed his way inside and found himself jammed in a solid mass of humanity. A vast crowd of grimy and excited steelworkers surrounded a makeshift platform at the end of the room. On it stood Irina. She looked small and frail, but her words had the power of a pile driver.

"Who wants to go on fighting this war?" yelled Irina.

"Nobody!" roared the crowd.

"Who wants a pack of fat, middle-class do-gooders running Russia?" asked Irina.

"Nobody!" answered the crowd.

"Well," said Irina, "what are we waiting for? Let's go and throw every last one of them out! They're waiting for us! Why don't we go and get them?"

"Right now!" called Sergei from the crowd.

A thousand voices took up the cry. "Right now! Right now! Right now!"

And the workers nearest the door began to surge out.

Now Indy was able to slip forward through the crowd. He leaped onto the platform and grabbed Irina by the arm. She looked at him in surprise.

"Indy, what are you doing here?"

"Trying to stop you from getting killed," said Indy, giving her a long, hard look. "Don't go."

"Don't go?" said Irina. "We've got these people fired up to take over the government of Russia. We're not pulling out now!"

"What's all this?" asked Sergei, climbing up onto the platform beside them.

"I've come here to tell you that if you march on the Tauride Palace now, you'll go down in a hail of bullets," said Indy. "They're ready for you."

"You're lying," said Sergei.

"You may have lied to me, Sergei," said Indy, "but I'm *not* lying to you."

"We lied to you, Comrade Spy," said Sergei, grabbing Indy angrily by the collar, "because you crossed the line. You tried to take advantage of our friendship to get information for your bosses. We had no choice."

Indy knew Sergei was right. Sergei and Irina might have betrayed their friendship. But in his eagerness to escape his basement desk, Indiana Jones had forced them to do so. It was a lesson he wouldn't forget.

"Okay," he said. "But that's not the point anymore. The point is that I *know* your revolution is going to fail."

"Come on," said Sergei. "How can you know something like that?"

"Because not even Lenin is backing it," Indy said. "We've been getting reports from all over the city. As of this moment, all the top Bolsheviks are out trying to hold the people back, make them go home. They know this isn't the right time."

"Maybe the men at the top are scared," said Irina. "Maybe they're too frightened to grab power while they've got the chance. But *we're* not."

"What about the Cossacks?" demanded Indy.

"The Cossacks!" said Sergei. "What *about* the Cossacks?"

"The Cossacks have come out in favor of the government," Indy said. "There are snipers on the rooftops along all the main roads."

Sergei and Irina were clearly taken aback. They didn't want to believe him.

"How do we know you're telling the truth?" said Sergei.

"Because I'm your friend," said Indy simply.

"But, Indy," argued Irina, "you work for a government that wants the revolution to fail. How can we believe you?"

"We have thirty thousand people here who'll

tip the balance between success and failure," said Sergei. "You think we're going to hold them back on your word?"

"On my word as your friend. Look—don't you see I'm trying to help you? Don't *do* this!" begged Indy, gesturing toward the crowd still pouring out of the room.

"I'm sorry, Indy," said Irina. "You're asking too much."

Indy realized it was useless to argue. The trust between them—their whole friendship—had crumbled into ruins. Without another word he stepped down off the platform and pushed his way through the crowd and out the door.

Chapter 12

At first glance the big, cluttered room looked deserted. The various young people who lived there had rushed out earlier in the day. Knapsacks, half-painted posters, and half-written letters lay where they had been left. Nothing moved.

There was no sound—except, perhaps, someone breathing. If you listened hard you would have heard that. And if you looked carefully, you would have seen Indy sitting in one of the big old armchairs. He was staring out the window at the rooftops of St. Petersburg, without seeing them. Lost in his thoughts, he took no notice as the door opened.

"Hello? Is anybody there?" asked Rosa. Since nobody replied, she came in and lit a lamp.

"Oh! Indy!" she cried out in surprise.

Indy looked at her silently. He felt too low to reply.

"I just came around because I've found some meat," said Rosa. "I was going to cook a stew and surprise everybody when they came back."

"Well, save yourself the trouble, Rosa," said Indy. "They're not coming back."

"Not coming back! What do you mean, Indy?"

"I mean that as we speak they're leading a pointless march of thousands of people right into an ambush by a regiment of Cossacks."

Rosa could hardly believe her ears.

"We've got to warn them!" she cried.

"I already did," answered Indy. "They didn't believe me because I work for the French government."

"But you're their friend," argued Rosa.

"Didn't count," said Indy.

"I guess you can't blame them," said Rosa, remembering the harsh scene that morning. "What are you going to do?"

"Do?" Indy said. "There's nothing I can do. I offered them what I had. They said no thanks. End of story."

"So they're going to die—for nothing," said Rosa.

"Probably," said Indy in despair.

Rosa's face suddenly became determined.

"Well, they're my friends and I'm not going to let that happen," she said.

Indy watched her leave and heard her feet clattering urgently down the stairs. But he just sat there without moving. Then his eyes strayed idly to Rosa's shopping bag. The tiny piece of meat had fallen out. Blood was oozing through the newspaper it was wrapped in. He watched as the blood dribbled onto the floor, wondering idly whether he should wipe it up.

Then at last something clicked in Indy's mind. Rosa was right. His friends might have rejected him, but that didn't mean he had to give up on them. That wasn't what friendship was about. He rushed to the window. Rosa, running hard, was at the corner, about to disappear into the maze of streets.

"Hey! Rosa!" he shouted. "Wait for me! I said wait for me!"

Then Indy was off and running!

When he caught up with Rosa, no words were needed. Rosa knew that Indy realized she'd been right. And both of them knew that whatever happened, they would always be friends.

Their racing footsteps echoed back and forth among the tall buildings. In the distance they could hear the faint sound of thousands of people singing the "Internationale"—the song of the workers. As they drew closer, they could gradually make out the words. The words were full of hope. They were the passionate words of people convinced they were marching toward a better life.

> *Arise ye slaves who know starvation.*
> *Shake off the curse that binds the earth!*
> *Our reason boils with indignation*
> *And makes us die to gain new birth!*

Suddenly Indy grabbed Rosa and pulled her into a doorway.

"What—?" asked Rosa, startled.

"Look up there—on the rooftops," said Indy.

Rosa saw a soldier. His machine gun was silhouetted against the bright evening sky. Her eyes scanned the roofline. There were dozens of soldiers, crouched behind their deadly weapons.

"They're on every rooftop in the street. They'll cut the marchers to pieces!" she exclaimed. "Indy, which way is the procession coming?"

"This way," said Indy.

They'd have to take a shortcut to get to the procession before it turned in to this street. Across from them, Indy could see the dark mouth of an alley. But the street was wide. If they tried to make a dash for it, the troops on the rooftops would see them for sure. He looked at Rosa. She understood.

"Shall we try it?" he asked.

Rosa looked at him, drew a deep breath, and gave a short nod.

"Okay," said Indy. "Let's go!"

They sprinted across the street in full view. There were shouts and then the *clunk-click* of a rifle getting ready to fire. The alley was just yards away. Indy grabbed Rosa's hand and threw them both toward its shelter. But the rain of bullets they had expected never fell.

They paused a few moments when they reached the alley. The words of the "Internationale" filled their ears:

We'll tear down our planet's false foundation
Then build a better world anew!
While he who lived in humble station
Will stand erect as is his due.

There was another shout from behind them. They started running again, their feet slipping on the paving stones. Suddenly they burst out into a square.

A huge procession was coming toward them. Tens of thousands of men, women, and children were on the march. Bobbing among them were hundreds of large banners and thousands of homemade placards calling for an end to war and the beginning of a bright new world. The sound of their singing flowed down the Nevsky Prospect like a river, carrying all before it.

Through conflict comes power.
Each will lift his face.
And thus will come to flower
At last—the human race!

Sergei and Irina were right at the head of the procession with their heads held high and their eyes shining. Leading them all, they held a red banner that said, "All Power to the People!" They looked like the vanguard of some new race. People who had put behind them the centuries of toil and oppression their forebears had known. The people of the future!

Indy and Rosa watched, deeply moved. And then Indy remembered why he and Rosa were there. He remembered the deadly silhouettes waiting on the rooftops just around the corner.

"Sergei! Irina! STOP! NOW!" he yelled, gesturing upward. "They're waiting for you!"

The great flood of singing was so overpowering it seemed as if no one would hear Indy's lone voice above the din. But Sergei did. He turned his head slowly, as if he were underwater. He saw Indy and smiled. Then he shook his head, as if rejecting Indy's message. He turned to face forward again, and led the procession toward the corner.

"Sergei! Irina! NO!" yelled Rosa.

But it was too late to stop them. The great torrent of people was flowing unstoppably into the ambush. For a second Indy hesitated—but only for a second. He was going to save his friends, whatever the risk. He started running, gathering speed with every stride, until he was moving faster than he ever had in his life. He reached the head of the procession just as it swung around the corner. Then he dove in a long, low arc toward Sergei and Irina.

In that split second the machine gunners on the rooftops opened fire. Bullets ricocheted from the surface of the road. People began to scream and hurl themselves to the ground. Banners collapsed over the jostling, struggling mass. The people behind, unaware of the attack, kept pouring around the corner into the street. A man clutched his chest and fell back into the crowd. A woman spun around again and again like a top, screaming, as bullets slammed into her, one after another.

Within seconds the procession was a rout. Indy had landed on the ground, half stunned. When his head cleared, he saw Sergei lying in the middle of the street. Blood was pouring from his chest, and his face was white.

Not far away, Irina rose groggily to her knees and looked around for Sergei.

"Sergei! Sergei!" she cried desperately. "Where are you?"

Indy rushed to Irina and pushed her down protectively, then helped her crawl over to Sergei. Struggling together amid the deafening din, they dragged him out of the line of fire.

Boris suddenly appeared at the edge of the seething crowd, clearing a way for Rosa. She ran forward to her wounded friend. Efficiently she ripped the clothes off Sergei's chest—and then stopped, shocked at what she saw. Sergei's chest was one massive wound. Indy held Irina as she cried out in terror.

"Sergei, Sergei! Don't die!" Irina begged. "It's all right. Rosa's here. She'll heal you. Look, she's got bandages. We'll get you to a hospital. Don't die, Sergei, don't die!"

Rosa was doing what she could to stop the flow of blood, but they all knew it was no use.

Sergei reached out and took Irina's hand. Then he saw Indy. Sergei was trying to say something. Indy bent closer to catch his words.

"So long, old friend," said Sergei in a soft mumble.

Indy nodded. "Friend." The circle was complete again.

Sergei's eyes rested on Irina. There was so much he wanted to say about the life they had planned.

"Irina," he said. "I always—"

But Sergei could get no further. His eyes widened in a sudden spasm of pain. Then his head fell back, his mouth still open.

He was dead.

Irina's wail of despair sounded through the square.

Indy and Rosa looked at each other. With Rosa's silent consent, Indy closed Sergei's eyes. Tears filled his own eyes. Rosa took Irina in her arms, as if to absorb some of her pain.

Boris leaped up and rushed back into the street. He shook his fist at the rooftops.

"Traitors! Traitors! Traitors!" he screamed at the top of his lungs.

But the massacre was over now. The marchers had fled. The troops were packing up their machine guns. No one was interested enough to shoot at the lone, defiant figure. It was all over. Boris's cries echoed into an empty silence.

Four hundred people died that day in July before the marchers realized the revolution wasn't going to happen yet. The Bolshevik leaders fled for their lives as government troops smashed their printing presses and closed their offices. For a time, the Bolsheviks were a broken force, and it seemed the threat of Communism was over.

Indy was busier than ever in the next few months, trying to keep track of everything that was going on. But his apartment was no longer a lively center of discussion and activity.

Numbed by grief, Irina left school and returned to her family. Dmitri disappeared altogether. Rosa's bright and trusting eyes grew listless with fatigue and sadness as she worked endless hours at the hospital. Even Boris was strangely quiet.

Meanwhile, the Bolsheviks pieced themselves together bit by bit, until the time was right to strike. When October came and snow fell again, they captured Russia in a single night.

In the years to come, whenever Indy thought about the Bolshevik Revolution, he didn't think of it in terms of Communism and capitalism. He didn't think about coups and countercoups. He thought about his friends—Rosa, Boris, and Dmitri. Most of all he thought about Sergei and Irina, and the wonderful new future they'd believed in so passionately. It was a future swept away in the treacherous tides of revolution—just as the paper boats that children put into water, carrying their dreams to some mysterious destination, are sometimes swamped and sunk by currents they did not even know existed.

Historical Note

The July Revolution of 1917 is one of the real mysteries of the Russian Revolution. Did the Bolshevik leaders plan it? Or did it just happen because ordinary people were so excited by the leaders' fiery speeches that they took events into their own hands?

Certainly Lenin did go to Finland just before the July Revolution began, rushing back to St. Petersburg when it was clear something important was going on. We also know that he was deeply uncertain about what to do when he returned. He was strongly tempted to go along with the people and overthrow the government. That would bring the Bolsheviks to power, all right. But how would the rest of the country react? And what about the army? Would it defend the Provisional Government or not? Lenin couldn't be sure. So the Bolshevik Party did not throw itself into the uprising.

In the hours after the marchers were massacred on the Nevsky Prospect, Lenin believed he was finished. Alexander Kerensky, the Minister of War, now had an excuse to crush the Bolsheviks once and for all. If he had done so, democracy might have won out in Russia at that time, and the history of the twentieth century would have been very different.

But Kerensky let the top leaders get away. Although the Bolsheviks were laid low, they had enough strength to recover and win the day that October. In fact, when they finally did make their bid for power, they had far fewer people on the streets of St. Petersburg than there had been in the uprising of July 3–5. A few thousand trained men seized the key points and held them. They didn't need the masses at all.

After that, Russia was fated to be the first great Communist state. Lenin was its first leader, and the country was reorganized into the Soviet Union. It was a giant experiment, using the ideas of Karl Marx, that lasted for most of the twentieth century. Communist rule brought civil war, mass starvation, labor camps for those who disagreed with the government, secret police, and the ruthless dictator Joseph Stalin, who took over when Lenin died. The experiment didn't end until the 1990s. By then the country was so bogged down in poverty and inefficiency that the leader of the Communist Party himself, Mikhail Gorbachev, at last admitted, "The model does not work."

But by then millions had suffered and died in an attempt to make it work. Such were the results of those fateful months in 1917, when Indiana Jones tried to help his friends . . . and the people of Russia tried, in vain, to take the future into their hands and make it better than the past.

A Note on St. Petersburg

"Peter's City" was renamed Petrograd in 1914 after Germany declared war on Russia. "Burg" is the German word for city, and the Russians did not want their capital to have a name that came from their enemy. After the Bolsheviks took over, the capital was moved to Moscow. Petrograd was renamed Leningrad in 1924 to honor Lenin. But it became St. Petersburg again in 1991, in memory of better days.

By any name, it remains a beautiful city.

TO FIND OUT MORE . . .

"Leningrad, Russia's Window on the West" by Howard LaFay. Published in *National Geographic*, May 1971. A brief history of the city, with an emphasis on contemporary life. See the palaces Indy saw when Leningrad was Petrograd. Maps and color photos.

Superpowers: The U.S.A., The U.S.S.R. (Imperial Visions: The Rise and Fall of Empires) by Max M. Mintz (The U.S.A.) and John Bennet (The U.S.S.R.). Published by HBJ Press, 1980. Includes lively accounts of how Trotsky, Lenin, and Stalin changed the face of Russia. Terrific paintings and photos, along with asides about Russian art, poetry, film, and propaganda, make the revolution come alive.

Lenin: Founder of the Soviet Union by Abraham Resnick. Published by Childrens Press, 1987. A detailed history of the greatest hero of the Soviet Union, the man that Indy's friends believed would revolutionize Russia with his convictions. Black-and-white photos.

Capitalism vs. Socialism: Economic Policies of the U.S. & the U.S.S.R. (An Economic Impact Book) by Michael Kronenwetter. Published by Franklin Watts, 1986. Explores the origins and concepts of the capitalist and socialist economic systems, then shows how they work in practice. A chapter describes the development of Communism, the Soviet Union's version of socialism, after the Russian Revolution of 1917.

Soviet Union . . . in Pictures (Visual Geography Series) by Stephen C. Feinstein. Published by Lerner Publications Company, 1989. A short survey of the country, packed with facts, maps, and photos (many in color). Perfect for a social studies report.

Journey to the Soviet Union by Samantha Smith. Published by Little, Brown and Company, 1985. See the Soviet Union through the eyes of a 10-year-old American girl who visited Moscow, Leningrad, and an international children's camp at the invitation of Soviet leader Yuri Andropov in 1983. Plenty of photos (some in color) and a text written in the first person add up to a fun and informative look at life a few years before the Soviet Union dissolved.

A Day in the U.S.S.R. Published by Collins Publishers, 1987. On May 15, 1987, prominent photojournalists from over twenty countries photographed whatever they wished throughout the fifteen republics of the Soviet Union. Full-color photographs with short captions show timeless landscapes that Indy might have seen, as well as modern-day people and places from Leningrad to Siberia.

Russian Folk Tales illustrated by Ivan I. Bilibin, translated by Robert Chandler. Published by Shambhala/Random House, 1980. A wonderful collection of seven traditional Russian stories that Indy's friends would have heard while growing up. Colorful illustrations throughout.